THE HOllOWING TRILOGY

KANTRELL YOUNG-WINTERS

Kantrell Young-Winters (b. 1982) is a creative force wrapped in mystery, ink, and imagination. Equal parts art lover and adrenaline junkie, she thrives where brushstrokes meet jump scares and plot twists. Whether she's sketching surreal dreamscapes, dissecting the psychology of a Hitchcock classic, or penning her own spine-tingling tales, Kantrell lives for the thrill of the unexpected.

A lifelong devotee of horror films and psychological thrillers, she doesn't just watch what she analyzes, questions, and rewrites endings in her head. Her mind is a maze of "what ifs" and "why nots," fueled by critical thinking and a deep love for storytelling that bites back.

When she's not writing with a vengeance or debating the symbolism in her favorite films, you'll find her haunting art galleries, sipping cold Sprite, and plotting her next creative conquest. Kantrell doesn't just consume culture, she crafts it, one eerie idea at a time.

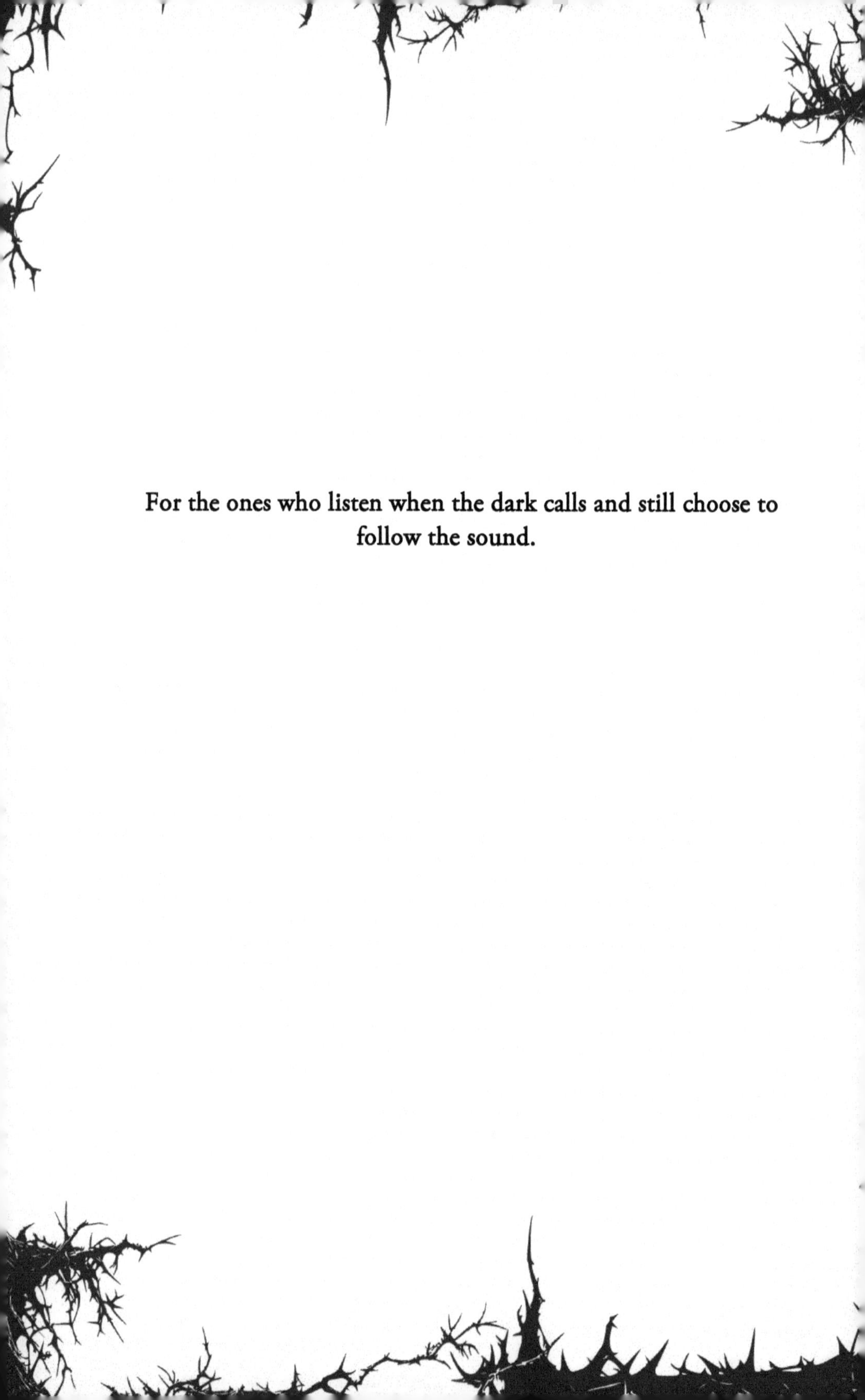

For the ones who listen when the dark calls and still choose to follow the sound.

THE
HOLLOWING

KANTRELL YOUNG-WINTERS

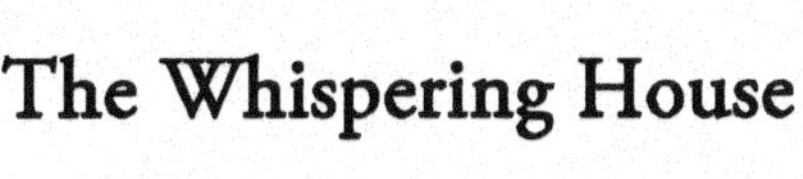

The Whispering House
Chapter One: Arrival

Dawn crawled over the horizon like an exhausted survivor. The sky above Ashmere Bay was bruised from grey to gold as Eva Maren's car wound along the coastal road. Sea fog clung to the cliffs, rolling in soft and heavy waves that swallowed the pines and telephone lines until the world narrowed to the hiss of her tires and the rhythmic pulse of the ocean below.

She had been driving for nearly four hours, and every mile farther from the city made her chest loosen, then tighten again. Freedom and fear—they felt almost identical now.

The sign appeared suddenly: ASHMERE BAY—POP. 1,427.

Someone had carved a jagged line through the number, as if even that was too many.

Eva slowed, taking in the view. Below her, the town was a crooked spill of rooftops, worn docks, and lantern-lit shops huddled against the sea. The kind of place that looked trapped in another decade, its salt-stained windows watching newcomers like they were a storm.

She had come here in silence, for a place to breathe.

But the email from Arc Light Productions had made it sound simpler than it was:

Blackthorn House requires an on-site evaluation before restoration can begin. The estate is fully secured. You'll have exclusive access for the first month.

She was a documentary filmmaker, not a ghost hunter—but lately, the lines between the two felt blurred. The last project she'd shot, *The Orphan's Choir*, had nearly broken her. The subjects, the stories, the sleepless nights.

She'd promised herself she'd never make another film about trauma.

Yet here she was, drawn to a decaying mansion by the edge of the sea—because something about the name *Blackthorn* had whispered to her in the way only trouble could.

Ashmere Bay itself felt alive.

The locals were up early, hauling nets, smoking outside dinner, staring just long enough to make her wonder what they saw. At the general store, she stopped for coffee and directions, and the woman at the counter—a grey-haired matron named Marla—blinked when Eva mentioned the estate.

"You're headed *up there*?" Marla asked. "Don't nobody stay long at Blackthorn."

Eva smiled politely, brushing it off as folklore. Every small town had its story.

Marla leaned closer, voice dropping.

"You'll hear it, you know. The house. Don't matter if you believe it or not."

Eva didn't ask what "it" meant. She just thanked her and left, though her hands trembled slightly as she opened the door.

The road to Blackthorn House was narrower, lined with trees that seemed to tilt inward, as if trying to warn her back. The GPS signal flickered and died.

And then she saw it.

The mansion rose from the fog like a cathedral to grief—sprawling stone wings, shuttered windows, and an iron gate half-consumed by vines. The sea roared behind it, its cliffs dark and jagged, and the gulls above cried like lost children.

The house wasn't empty. She could *feel* that before she even crossed the gate.

It wasn't that someone was watching it; it was that the air itself seemed to hold memory, thick and restless.

Inside, the scent of old salt and cedar rot hit her. Dust motes spun in the slanted light from broken windows. The grand staircase loomed; its rail polished smoothly from centuries of hands. Every sound she made came back twice—an echo and an answer.

Eva set down her camera bag, checked her recorder, and whispered a test:

"Day one. Arrival at Blackthorn House. Property sealed, remote access offline. Initial impression—"

A whisper slid through the room.

No wind. Not settling beams. A voice—soft and distant, impossible to place.

You came back.

Eva froze.

The recorder light blinked red.

And though the voice was gone, the air felt heavier now—as if the house itself was breathing with her.

Evening draped itself over Blackthorn House like a shroud.

By the time Eva finished unpacking, the sea had turned to molten slate beneath the twilight. The house moaned with each gust of wind that rolled in from the cliffs—long, low sounds that could have been breath, or memory, or both.

She set up her camera tripod in the foyer, aligning it toward the staircase, where the light from the chandelier fractured against the dust. It would make good b-roll footage: *empty, atmospheric, haunted by time.*

But as she reviewed the frame through the viewfinder, her brow furrowed.

There was movement.

A soft flicker, like someone descending the stairs—but when she looked up, the staircase was still. Empty. The kind of emptiness that hummed.

She zoomed in.

Nothing. Just the warped outline of the banister, and the faint reflection of her own silhouette in the lens.

"You're letting this place get to you," she murmured to herself, and hit *record.*

Later, in what had once been the library, Eva discovered the first of many curiosities.

Most of the furniture was sheeted, except for one armchair near the fireplace—a deep crimson relic with clawed feet. On the small side table besides, it sat a single object: a porcelain teacup.

The liquid inside had long since evaporated, leaving only a ring of brown residue.

But it was the placement that unnerved her—centered perfectly, as if waiting for someone's return.

She reached out to move it, then hesitated. The porcelain was warm.

And from the hall, something creaked.

Eva turned off the camera light, holding her breath.

The dark swallowed everything.

There it was again—a *dragging* sound, slow and deliberate, from the floor above.

Something heavy being pulled across the wood.

Her rational mind snapped into gear, houses settle, animals wander, pipes groan, but the sound wasn't mechanical. It was purposeful.

"Probably a loose shutter," she whispered, as if saying it aloud could make it true.

But even as she said it, she knew. The noise wasn't coming from the outside walls. It was coming from the hallway that ran directly above her.

She grabbed her flashlight. Each step up the grand staircase creaked underfoot, announcing her ascent. The beam of light trembled slightly in her grip.

The corridor stretched long and narrow, lined with portraits of strangers whose eyes gleamed faintly when the light passed over them. One painting had been slashed clean through, the tear exposing the faded wallpaper beneath.

The dragging sound had stopped.

But in its place came another—soft weeping, just barely audible.

Eva froze.

It was coming from the last room on the right, the one with the door slightly ajar.

She edged closer, her breath shallow, and pushed it open.

Inside was a child's bedroom, untouched by time: a small iron bed, a cracked mirror, wallpaper of faded moons and stars. The sound had stopped the moment she entered.

Only the curtains moved now, swaying though the window was closed.

Eva lowered her flashlight and exhaled.

"Just wind," she muttered. "Old houses always—"

The mirror screamed.

Not a human sound—more like glass grinding against itself, high and shrill. Eva stumbled back, the flashlight falling from her hand, spinning across the floor. The reflection in the mirror twisted, the room behind her *warping* in impossible angles—the bed stretching, the shadows deepening until a figure seemed to stand just behind her shoulder.

A child's voice whispered, so close it brushed her ear:

Why did you leave me here?

Eva turned—no one.

When she looked back, the mirror was still.

Her reflection stared back, trembling, alone.

Two hours later, she sat on the porch with her laptop, typing up her field notes with shaking hands. The rational part of her wanted to document it— light distortion, auditory hallucination, residual trauma projection.

But another part—the part that had learned to trust her instincts after years of filming the unexplainable—knew better.

This wasn't a projection. It was an *invitation.*

From inside, a faint melody began to play. A piano. Slow, mournful.

Eva's head snapped up. She hadn't restored power to the generator.

The melody drifted through the open windows, sweet and deliberate — the kind of tune someone plays when they know they're being listened to.

Eva stepped inside, following the sound to the parlor. The piano stood there, its keys yellowed, its lid heavy with dust. The bench was empty.

But the keys moved.

Not all of them—just enough to carry the tune.

E-flat. D. G. B.

Repeatedly. Like a memory being practiced.

Her camera was still rolling in the foyer. When she reviewed the footage later that night, the image showed something she hadn't noticed:

As she entered the parlor, a shape rose from the piano bench—tall, thin, colorless—and dissolved into the shadowed corner before she crossed the threshold.

She watched the frame five times, each slower than the last, until the truth of it began to sink into her bones.

Blackthorn House wasn't just haunted. It was awake.

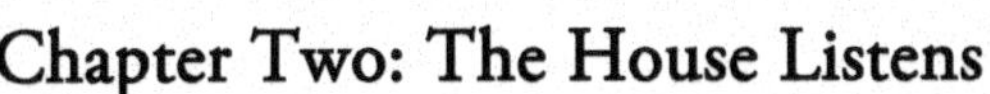

Chapter Two: The House Listens

The storm arrived before sunset, sweeping inland from the sea with the heavy scent of brine and ozone. By the time Eva finished unpacking her camera equipment, the fog that had haunted the cliffs all day had thickened into a curtain of rain. Blackthorn House moaned against the wind like an old ship straining in its mornings.

She set her tripod near the grand staircase. The foyer was vast enough to swallow her voice, and the sweep of her flashlight caught glints of tarnished brass and the cracked face of a grandfather clock that hadn't ticked in decades.

"Day one, 8:13 P.M.," she said into her recorder. "Weather worsening. Power steady for now. No visible signs of recent maintenance. House feels… restless."

The last word left her lips reluctantly. Restless was for people, not buildings.

When she replied to the clip to check the levels, she heard her own voice clear and crisp—followed by a whisper that wasn't hers.

Help me

She froze. Rewound. Played again.

Nothing. Only static and the thrum of the rain.

"Great," she muttered, setting the recorder aside. "Already imagining things."

She made her way through the first floor: a study lined with shelves warped by damp, a music room with an overturned harp, a dining hall where the ceiling had half-collapsed to reveal an attic she wasn't ready to explore.

The kitchen was the only room that felt remotely alive. Someone had covered the counters with sheets that smelled faintly of lemon oil. A single porcelain teacup rested in the sink, clean but chipped.

Eva filled the kettle, but when she went to light the stove, the flame refused to catch. She sighed, pouring the water into a thermos instead.

Her laptop chimed with a low-battery warning. She'd meant to plug it in earlier, but most of the outlets were dead. Only the one in the parlor seemed to work.

That was when she heard it: three slow knocks from somewhere upstairs.

She froze mid-step. The sound was deliberate, measured—not the groan of timber or shifting pipes.

Knock. Knock. Knock.

"Hello?"

Her voice echoed through the house and returned in fragments.

lo... lo... Only the echo answered her back.

No answer.

She grabbed her flashlight and scanned the staircase. The beam trembled slightly in her hand.

"Probably loose shutters," she whispered, more to convince herself than anything.

The knocking stopped.

By the time she reached the landing, the air had cooled, dense with the scent of rain seeping through the roof. Her light caught the edge of a door slightly ajar at the end of the hall.

The brass nameplate read: The Library.

Inside, rows of books leaned like weary sentinels. Dust hung thick as cobweb silk. But it wasn't the books that made her breath hitch—it was the massive portrait above the fireplace.

A man in Victorian dress stared out, his face long and pale, his eyes painted with unnerving precision. Beneath the frame, the nameplate read: Jonathan Blackthorn, 1856–1912.

Eva lifted her camera and snapped a photo. The flash burst against the room's darkness—and for an instant, she thought the man in the painting smiled.

The thunder outside cracked like bone.

She found a desk under the window and brushed away the dust. Beneath her fingertips, she discovered a small brass plate etched into the wood:

To preserve is to remember. Remembering is to live forever.

A tingle crept down her spine.

She opened the desk drawer. Inside lay a collection of phonograph cylinders, each carefully labeled in spidery handwriting:

- Exp. 1: Retention

- Exp. 2: Amnesia

- Exp. 3: Revival

Her pulse quickened. She hadn't seen anything about these in the archives.

She set her recorder beside the drawer. "Found a series of phonograph experiments. Possibly recordings made by Jonathan Blackthorn himself."

When she stopped speaking, the recorder kept going—a faint shuffle, a whisper, and then her *own voice*, replying from the device:

"Don't open the third one."

Eva's throat closed.

She stared at the recorder. The indicator light blinked steadily.

"Playback," she whispered.

But on playback, there was nothing. Only the sound of the rain.

The storm worsened after midnight. The wind slammed against the shutters like a giant's fist, and the sea could be heard from miles inland—a low, unending roar. Eva set her recorder on the desk beside the phonograph.

The machine was a relic: brass horn, cracked mahogany base, and a hand crank that resisted every turn. The cylinders were labeled with meticulous care, the ink brown with age.

She hesitated before selecting Exp. 1—Retention.

"Let's see what secrets you're keeping, Mr. Blackthorn," she murmured.

The needle dropped.

At first, there was only static—the hiss and pop of wax and dust. Then a man's voice emerged, warped but unmistakably deliberate.

"Experiment one. Subject responds to auditory stimulus. Memory retention at seventy-two percent. The process continues. The house remembers."

A faint *scraping* echoed in the background of the recording—like something heavy dragging across wood.

Eva turned toward the far side of the library. Nothing moved. Yet she could have sworn one of the tall ladders had shifted an inch closer.

The voice continued:

"To preserve thought is to trap it. The walls absorb what the mind releases."

The phonograph crackled, then fell silent.

She checked the clock on her phone—12:43 A.M.

Her reflection in the library window startled her; the lightning made it appear as though someone else stood just behind her shoulder.

Eva spun around.

Nothing. Only shelves, shadows, and the portrait of Jonathan Blackthorn, now barely visible in the storm's flashes.

When she faced the window again, her reflection *wasn't alone.*

A man's outline, faint as mist, stood beside her in the glass. His mouth moved, but no sound came.

The phonograph needle lifted itself with a *click.*

Without warning, it began to play again—this time a woman's voice, trembling:

"Please, Jonathan… stop the recordings. The voices don't sleep anymore."

The ghostly reflection turned its head toward Eva.

She staggered back, knocking into a chair. "What—"

The phonograph's horn emitted a sharp squeal, then went silent.

The reflection vanished.

But now the whisper came from *behind* her, soft and unmistakable:

"He never stopped."

Heart in her throat, she fled the library, clutching the flashlight in her trembling hand. Its beam jittered wildly, casting ominous shadows along the corridor's cracked wallpaper. She gulped as the realization hit her—the house was shifting. The creaking around her grew louder, almost alive.

Doors she could have sworn were open were now firmly shut, and the hallway seemed to stretch endlessly ahead. It felt as though she were trapped in a loop, running and running, yet getting nowhere.

When she finally burst into the foyer, the grandfather clock stood upright again. Its pendulum swung, slow and deliberate, even though she knew it had been frozen when she arrived.

Tick.

Tock. Tick. Tock.

The sound filled the entire house.

She clutched her recorder.

"This is Eva Maren," she said, breathless. "Blackthorn House appears to be… responding. The clock in the foyer is functioning without power. I repeat: the house is active."

Her own voice replayed instantly from the recorder, though she hadn't pressed playback.

"The house is listening, Eva."

Her blood turned to ice, and chills curled up her spine.

The lights flickered once—and then the power went out.

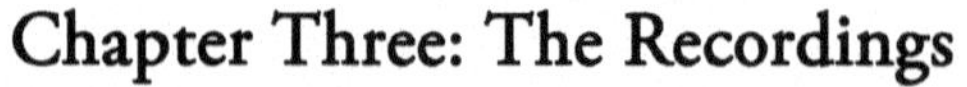

Chapter Three: The Recordings

The storm refused to relent.

Rain battered the glass with a rhythm that seemed to echo her racing pulse. The candles she'd lit now burned low, their wax pooling like small, molten eyes on the table beside her. The generator refused to start, leaving only the deep, uneven breaths of the storm as company.

Eva had locked herself in the parlor. The phonograph sat across from her, the second cylinder glinting faintly in the candlelight. Exp. 2: Amnesia.

She told herself she wouldn't play it. She told herself she'd wait until morning, until the power returned, until logic could anchor her again. And yet—her hands betrayed her.

The cylinder slid onto the spindle.

The crank turned.

The needle dropped.

Static.

Then silence.

Then—

"Experiment two. Memory extraction unsuccessful. Subject resists erasure. Voices remain. Recommend isolation."

The voice was Jonathan Blackthorn again, measured and clinical, but with something unsteady creeping beneath the precision.

"The dead recall what the living forgets. Perhaps that is the key."

Eva frowned, pen poised above her notepad. "Extraction? Voices?" she whispered, writing as she listened.

Then came another voice—softer, wet, as if spoken from behind a wall. *"Jonathan, please. You said I'd sleep."*

Eva froze. Her eyes darted to the door.

The voice wasn't coming from the phonograph anymore. It was inside the *room*.

"You said I'd sleep…"

The candle nearest the window flickered violently, then went out, extinguished by an invisible gust. The remaining flames leaned away from the sound, as if recoiling.

Eva forced herself to breathe. "Who's there?"

The response came not from the air—but from the walls.

A slow, deliberate whisper that vibrated through the plaster:

"You shouldn't have played it."

The phonograph spun faster on its own, the cylinder whirring until the machine screamed with friction. Eva lunged forward to stop it—and as her fingers touched the crank, the needle *snapped*.

The phonograph fell silent.

And then came the voice of Jonathan again—not from the machine this time, but from directly behind her ear:

"You woke her."

The house is awakened. At once, it feels like the rooms are opening and closing on their own—the hardwood creaking of the staircase, of the lounge, the room above, the windows groaning as if someone is knocking from outside.

Then, footsteps outside the parlor. Pacing as if agitated.

Inside the parlor, the portraits seemed to shift their expressions under the lightning's pulse—the smiles turning into grimaces, almost pulled down forcefully into a horrifying arch. Their eyes turned down. Even the wallpaper, pale blue with silver lines, began to ripple as if alive.

The temperature dropped so suddenly that her breath turned white. She reached for her recorder, hit "playback" —but her voice was gone. Every file on the device now contained the same hiss, the same faint sound: someone breathing.

As if someone was standing close enough to fog the microphone.

Eva backed toward the door. It refused to open. The knob turned freely, but the wood stayed locked in place. Behind her, the phonograph needle lifted itself again.

The third cylinder—Exp. 3: Resurrection—rolled from the shelf and landed at her feet.

Her recorder clicked on by itself.

A single phrase came through, spoken in her own voice, though she hadn't said it yet:

"It has already begun."

****

When morning finally came, the storm had passed—but the house hadn't changed back.

Every window was fogged from the inside.

Every mirror was cracked.

And the front door, which she'd left bolted, now hung open.

Outside, her car sat just as she'd left it—except for the mud on the windshield.

Someone—or something—had traced a single word with a finger:

STAY.

Eva looked back toward Blackthorn House. From one of the top windows, a shadow moved.

Not a flicker of wind or a trick of light—something watching her. Waiting.

And when she raised her recorder to document it, the device began to record on its own.

The red light blinked.

Then her own voice whispered through:

"You can leave, but she won't."

— ◆ —

Chapter Four: The Resurrection Room

The stairs weren't there before.

At least—that's what Eva told herself as she stared at the gaping void behind the library's east wall. The wallpaper peeled back like torn skin, exposing a narrow stone passage that descended into darkness. A damp, metallic smell drifted upward—something between rust and rot.

She flicked on her flashlight. The beam trembled. Stone steps spiraled down into a throat of black.

Her voice recorder clicked on as she spoke, steady despite the hammering in her chest.

"Entry Log 04. Discovered hidden access behind the bookshelf. Descending. The air temperature is below 50 degrees. Smells organic… possibly decomposing matter."

The steps ended at a heavy iron door. Its hinges glistened with oil. She pressed a hand to the handle—warm to the touch. The door *opened itself.*

What lay beyond looked nothing like a basement.

It was a laboratory.

Glass cylinders lined the walls, each filled with amber fluid and fragments of anatomy—hands, eyes, spinal cords coiled like serpents. Tubes snaked across the floor, leading into a central tank large enough to hold a body.

Above it, a mechanical rig hung suspended: gears, pulleys, electrodes. A sign etched into the steel read:

Exp. 3: Resurrection.

Eva whispered the word aloud, barely able to hear herself.

Her light drifted to the far wall, where dozens of *photographs* had been pinned—the same woman, her face serene and pale. One photo bore a handwritten note:

"Elena—Day 47. Response achieved."

Eva's stomach turned. "Elena Blackthorn," she murmured. "The wife."

Beneath the photos lay a table. Upon it rested another phonograph cylinder, sealed in glass.

Exp. 4: Reanimation. The last recording

She hesitated, then lifted the lid.

The voice was not Jonathan's this time. It was Elena's—faint, but unmistakably human.

"Jonathan, it's dark. Please... stop this."

Then Jonathan's voice, sharp, desperate:

*"You came back, Elena! You **spoke!**"*

"No. Not me... not anymore."

Static roared. Then a new sound emerged—a wet, rhythmic pulse, like something breathing through liquid.

The tank at the room's center began to hum.

Eva turned slowly toward it as the liquid inside started to move—bubbles rising from the murky depths. Something pale floated upward, pressing against the glass.

A *face.*

Eyes open, unblinking.

The mouth moved.

Not speaking—*mimicking.*

It was mouthing the words of the recording.

"Not me... not anymore..."

The pressure in the room shifted, air compressing as though the walls were inhaling. The fluid in the tank drained suddenly, gurgling through hidden pipes, revealing the full figure of a woman—skin sewn in patches, wires running along her spine like veins of copper.

Her eyes snapped toward Eva.

And she smiled.

The lights overhead flickered to life, one by one, flooding the room with a sterile glow, but flickering still, casting eerie shadows on the pale figure.

Eva stumbled backward. The machinery screamed—pistons firing, gears spinning, lightning crackling through coils.

Elena Blackthorn—or what remained of her—stepped free from the tank. Her movements were disjointed, puppet-like, yet graceful in a terrible way.

Her lips parted. "You played it again." Then her lips pulled down into a smile.

Eva ran. Her footfalls thumped on the hardwood.

The stairwell slammed shut behind her as she reached it. The air above rippled like heat on asphalt, and suddenly she was no longer in the same corridor. The mansion's walls had shifted. The paintings now depicted faces she didn't recognize—*her own among them.*

Every exit was gone.

Horrified and panting, she collapsed against a mirror in the hall—the same cracked one she'd seen earlier. This time, it was whole.

Her reflection stared back with wide, terrified eyes.

Then it smiled—half a second later, her own face was far from smiling.

Her reflection lifted the recorder to its lips. Eva hadn't moved.

It spoke in her own voice, soft and almost tender:

"The house remembers everyone who listens."

A faint crack split the silence. The mirror fractured down the center, dividing her face into two uneven halves. Then the reflection reached its hand toward the glass.

Eva froze, eyes wide with terror, as from behind the shimmering surface something pressed forward—the reflection's pale hand, trembling yet deliberate. The glass seemed to bend under the pressure, groaning as if alive.

Eva screamed as the hand burst through, shards scattering like snow, glittering in the flicker of the dying light.

And from the broken mirror's depth came the whisper of Jonathan Blackthorn, so close it burned:

"Elena needed a vessel."

The reflection's eyes—*her* eyes—bled black.

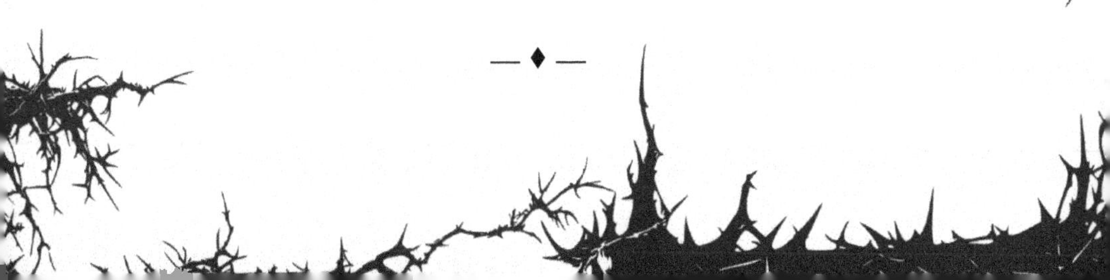

— ◆ —

Chapter Five: The Hollowing Begins

"Some houses don't remember—they hunger."

"Sound remembers what sight forgets.

If a house listens long enough, it begins to dream—and in its dreaming, it becomes alive." - Jonathan Blackthorn's Journal.

Previously in The Hollowing…

Documentary filmmaker Eva Maren arrived at Blackthorn House to capture its history but uncovered something far older and hungrier than ghosts. The house recorded memory itself, turning voices into echoes that could never die. When she descended into the Resurrection Room, the walls whispered her name—and the house began to breathe.

****

[REC 02:14 a.m.]

The dark was absolute.

Eva's first thought wasn't *"Where am I?"* But *why is it so quiet?* The generator should have been humming below the floorboards, that constant metallic drone she'd come to depend on. Instead, there was only the shallow rise and fall of her own breath.

The camera's red light blinked once in the black—a dying heartbeat. She reached for it blindly, fingers brushing the lens, and froze. The metal was *warm.*

Not from her touch. From something inside.

[REC 02:15 a.m.]

Something brushed past her ear.

Not air, not movement—*sound.* A single low hum like a cello string drawn slowly, trembling in the dark. Eva's pulse answered it. The camera's light blinked again, weaker this time.

She pushed herself up. Her palm met the cold floorboards; they were slick with condensation. She remembered the storm that had rolled in before she lost power, but this wasn't rain. The boards pulsed faintly, as if there was water moving beneath them.

****

[REC 02:18 a.m.]

"Hello?" Her voice came out raw. Playback static crackled from the recorder on her shoulder, the one she hadn't turned off. Her voice repeated itself back to her—distorted, too close to the mic.

"Hello?"

"—llo?"

"—lo?"

Then a breath that wasn't hers.

She froze.

The camera in her hands vibrated, a small mechanical shudder that sounded like a sigh.

****

[REC 02:22 a.m.]

She reached for the camera light and clicked it once.

A cone of pale red spilled across the hall—except it wasn't the hall. The doorway she'd crawled through was gone. Where the threshold had been, there was now a narrow corridor lined with mirrors, each one cloudy, as if painted over from the inside.

She whispered to the recorder: "This… this isn't my layout. This isn't my layout."

Her breath fogged the nearest glass. For a moment, the fog didn't clear. It shivered, then moved backward, retreating *into* the mirror. Something on the other side was breathing with her.

The camera caught a reflection: the beam from its own light bouncing down the corridor like a heartbeat. But in the playback screen, the light pulsed slower—off-sync, as if the reflection had its own rhythm.

****

[REC 02:27 a.m.]

A door at the far end creaked open. Eva steadied the camera, every muscle in her arm shaking. The lens refused to focus; static crackled in its internal mic.

When she tried to zoom, the focus wheel turned *on its own.*

She should have run then.

Instead, she whispered, "Show me," and the corridor obeyed.

****

[REC 02:30 a.m.]

The hallway smelled of turpentine and wet plaster. Eva's shoes left faint red prints on the boards—paint, not blood, but too thick, too fresh. She moved toward the open door, camera light trembling across the walls.

The air pressed close, humid and heavy, and with every step, the mirrors along the corridor cleared just enough to show her passing.

None of them showed her face.

At the end of the hall hung a portrait she hadn't seen before: a woman at an easel, brush poised above a canvas that glowed faintly even in the red light. The plaque beneath read: **ELENA BLACKTHORN, 1892.**

The woman's painted eyes followed Eva's movement. When she lifted the camera, the lens filled with static—no image, only a brief flash of her own reflection staring back from inside the portrait, holding a camera that wasn't there.

****

[REC 02:33 a.m.]

She whispered, "Jonathan said you never finished your work." The audio spiked. On playback, a whisper layered over hers:

"Neither did you."

The lights in the hallway blinked one by one, each bulb flickering with the same rhythm as her heartbeat. The hum returned beneath the floorboards, louder now, tied to the lights. The corridor was pulsing.

****

In the studio beyond the portrait, easels stood in a perfect circle. Each held a half-finished painting: the same image repeated—a figure crouched on the floor, camera in hand, caught mid-scream. The walls were covered in soundproof foam, but it was torn and warped as if it had swollen and burst from within.

Eva turned the camera toward the ceiling. The microphones she had hung earlier now dangled on their cords like vines. They were swaying gently, though there was no draft.

[REC 02:41 a.m.]

She heard the first breath again. It came from the speaker array in the corner—her own voice, recorded earlier that day: *"If a house listens long enough…"*

The next line didn't belong to her: *"…it begins to dream."*

The walls contracted. Paint cracked in spider-web patterns that met above her head. A fine dust rained down. Somewhere behind the mirrors, something shifted—a wet, deliberate sound like lungs filling.

Eva steadied the camera, forcing the words out:

"This is Eva Maren, inside Blackthorn House. There's movement inside the walls. It's responding to sound. Maybe vibration. Maybe…"

The floor groaned. The recording glitched. On the screen, her timestamp looped backward three seconds, then forward again. The house was *editing* her.

She went back toward the door. The portrait of Elena was still there, but the canvas had changed. The painted woman was gone; in her place was a mirror of black glass. Eva's reflection stood inside it, eyes open wide, camera lifted, the red light now on the *other* side.

"Stop," she whispered, but the reflection kept filming.

[REC 02:48 a.m.]

The hum beneath the floor resolved into words. They weren't spoken to, they were *remembered*: voices layered together, centuries of recordings bleeding through the wood. She recognized her own voice among them, calling from somewhere deep in the house.

Her knees gave out. The camera hit the floor with a dull thud but kept rolling. In the lens, light swam and folded like water. The corridor behind her stretched farther, each mirror blooming open into a dark frame that breathed.

A final whisper, close enough to fog the glass of the lens:

"The Hollowing had begun long before she arrived. She was just the next sound it wanted to remember."

The camera light blinked once, twice—then went dark.

— ◆ —

Chapter Six: The House Breathes

[REC 03:01 a.m.]

Darkness again, but this time it's moving.

The camera had shut itself off at 2:49 A.M. when the lights died. Now it clicked back on without her touch. Eva lay on the floor of the studio, cheek against cold wood. Every plank rose and fell beneath her in slow, tidal swells. The house was breathing.

She whispered, "Testing—testing—"

The microphone answered in kind: *Testing—testing*—followed by a third voice, slightly delayed:

Eva… Eva…

She sat up, head pounding. The air felt thick, as if she were underwater. Each inhale carried the metallic tang of rust and salt. Her ears popped. Far off, the sea hammered the cliffs outside, but its rhythm matched the pulse of the floor.

[REC 03:07 a.m.]

She found the stairs twisted in the wrong direction. The banister leaned inward toward the hall, warped into the curve of a ribcage. The wallpaper—Elena's favorite maroon damask—had split down the center like a seam, exposing plaster that pulsed faintly in time with her heartbeat.

She filmed as she climbed. Each step exhaled beneath her foot. A draft hissed between the walls, not cold but warm—body heat. At the landing, a door was ajar that hadn't been there before.

****

Inside was Jonathan's study. Or what *used* to be his study. The desk sat at the center, and on it her camera feed played from a dozen monitors, each at a different delay. She watched herself enter the room seconds after she had. The screens flickered between past and present, like the house was running surveillance on time itself.

Eva whispered, "Jonathan, what did you build here?" A whisper from the speaker: *A mirror that listens.*

She turned slowly. A phonograph stood in the corner; the horn aimed directly at her. The needle lowered itself and a recording began to play—a woman's voice, distant and calm:

"Elena Blackthorn, Session 7. Subject responds to reflection stimuli. Memory retention measured through echo decay."

Then another voice, her own, layered in after Elena's:

"Session 8. Subject Eva Maren. Echo decay is unstable. Subject recording continues."

[REC 03:15 a.m.]

Her blood iced. She'd never made that entry.

The phonograph needle scraped forward on its own, and the recording changed:

"Subject integration commencing."

The desk drawers slid open.

Inside lay reel-to-reel tapes labeled only with dates—the last one marked *Tomorrow.*

****

The floor beneath the study heaved. Dust fell from the rafters like ash. Through the window, she saw the trees outside bending toward the house, branches clawing at the glass. The sound was no longer wind; it was breathing—synchronized, collective, coming from every direction.

[REC 03:22 a.m.]

Eva backed against the wall.

Her camera light stuttered, illuminating slivers of writing carved into the plaster:

THE HOUSE IS A LUNG

THE AIR IS A VEIN

THE VOICE IS A DOOR

She raised the lens closer. Each word sank deeper into the wall as she read it, the letters closing like wounds. Something behind the plaster moaned.

She turned to run, but the doorway was gone. The wall had sealed shut, her reflection smeared across its surface like wet paint. The air thickened, pressing her flat. For a heartbeat, she saw faces moving in the grain of the wood—Jonathan, Elena, strangers—each exhaling in unison.

The camera slipped from her hands and landed on its side, recording the floorboards rising and falling. Her own breath synced with the rhythm until she couldn't tell which belonged to her.

Then, silence. A drawn, held breath that lasted far too long.

[REC 03:30 a.m.]

The wall opened again with a wet gasp. Eva stumbled through into the hall, coughing. Her reflection followed half a beat behind, mimicking the motion but not the expression. Its eyes stayed fixed on her even when she looked away.

She whispered, "It's awake."

And the hallway answered with a single, low inhale that shook the house to its foundation.

— ♦ —

Chapter Seven: Through the Walls

[REC 03:41 a.m.]

The light from her camera cut through dust thick as fog. The staircase she'd just descended was gone, the walls closing in behind her until the passage narrowed to shoulder width. The sound of breathing came not from the house now but from *within the walls themselves.*

Eva ran her hand along the plaster; it was warm, tacky, alive. Under her fingertips, something pulsed—a steady, slow rhythm like a heartbeat measured in centuries. The wood vibrated faintly beneath her touch.

"Recording continuously," she said, voice shaking. "I think… the structure's changed again. Every exit has folded back into itself."

[REC 03:45 a.m.]

She raised the camera. The lens focused on a split in the plaster—an uneven line no wider than a finger. When she pressed her ear to it, she heard whispers layered over one another: *her own voice,* reciting her notes, then laughter, then crying. The sounds bled together into a language without words, a chorus of half-remembered dreams.

The crack widened. Dust poured out in a fine stream, coating her sleeve. The voices became clear.

"Eva." The voice reached her in a whisper.

"Keep filming."

Her pulse stuttered. She backed away, but the floor beneath her shifted, the boards curved inward like the slope of a throat.

[REC 03:48 a.m.]

The air thinned. She aimed the camera upward. Above her, the ceiling flexed as if something large was crawling just on the other side.

Footsteps—bare, deliberate—traveled across the beams. They stopped directly above her head.

She whispered, "Jonathan?"

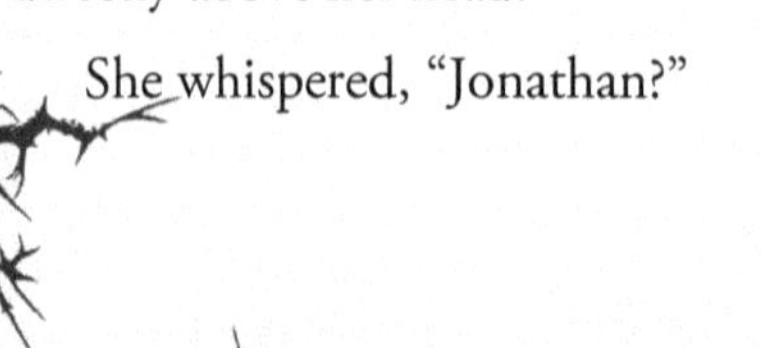

The house answered with the sound of a door opening somewhere deep below.

****

[REC 03:52 a.m.]

She followed the sound through a narrow corridor that hadn't existed before. The walls were stitched with wiring—copper veins that pulsed dimly with light. Every few feet, a speaker was mounted into the plaster, old and dust-coated. Each emitted faint static, punctuated by bursts of her own breathing.

She passed one and heard a recording from two hours earlier, her voice saying, *"Hello?"*

The same word she'd spoken in the dark at 2:18 A.M.

Another speaker whispered something new:

"You're almost inside."

Eva pressed the recorder close. "Inside what?"

The response came from every speaker at once:

"Inside us."

The corridor trembled. Paint peeled from the walls in curling strips, revealing layers of older wallpaper beneath—each patterned with faces blurred as though caught mid-scream.

****

[REC 03:59 a.m.]

At the corridor's end, she found a door labeled *ARCHIVE*. The brass handle burned cold under her hand. When she pushed it open, rows of reel-to-reel machines filled the space like pews in a chapel. Every machine spun slowly, the magnetic tape glinting as it looped through.

Each reel was marked with a name—dozens, maybe hundreds. Some she recognized: past owners, caretakers, researchers. Others were blank. One, near the center, bore her name: **EVA MAREN**.

Her stomach lurched. The tape on her reel wasn't black like the others; it shimmered faintly, translucent red. The reel rotated once, twice, then stopped.

Playback clicked on by itself. Her own voice filled the room:

"If you find this, don't listen. Don't let it hear you."

The machines all started spinning at once. The air filled with a mechanical drone that resolved into words: *"Through the walls, through the walls…"* repeated, faster, louder, until the sound became a single long note that shook the floor.

[REC 04:05 a.m.]

She covered her ears. The tape reels whirled faster, unwinding themselves. Strips of film snapped free and lashed across the room like tendrils. One brushed her arm; the skin beneath burned with sudden cold. When she looked, the mark it left behind was a line of text pressed into her flesh: *SESSION 9.*

She screamed. The microphones in the ceiling captured it and fed it back to her an instant later, layered and multiplied until it became an unbroken tone. The entire room shuddered; the machines bent inward, their metal casings twisting like ribs collapsing.

Eva bolted for the door—but the doorway had sealed into smooth plaster. She pounded against it.

The recordings slowed, their tone dropping into a steady, throbbing pulse.

From somewhere behind her, the voice of Elena Blackthorn spoke—not a recording this time, but a presence, calm and near.

"We gave it breath. You gave it voice. Now it will remember."

****

[REC 04:12 a.m.]

The reels stopped. Silence. Then, faintly, the scrape of a needle finding its groove. A new sound played: the heartbeat of the house, amplified, deliberate. With every thud, the walls expanded and contracted.

Eva pressed herself flat, camera shaking.

The heartbeat paused. A whisper threaded through the static:

"Breathe."

The walls inhaled. Air rushed from the floor vents, pulling her forward. She stumbled toward the center of the room, where a single circular panel waited—metal, polished, wet. The surface rippled as if it were liquid. She reached out without meaning to.

The panel pulsed once beneath her palm. Warm. Alive.

A face broke the surface—her own, eyes open, mouth moving though she heard no words. Then the voice came through the speakers again, quieter now:

"Through the walls."

The floor dropped.

Darkness swallowed her whole.

— ◆ —

Chapter Eight: The Hollowing

[REC 04:17 a.m.]

Darkness again, but thinner this time, like the air itself had been scraped raw.

Eva opened her eyes and found herself lying inside the walls.

The wood around her glistened with a slow pulse of light, veins of red threading through beams that were no longer beams but cartilage. Her camera hung from its strap, the lens cracked, still filming.

She whispered, "I'm inside it."

Playback answered, *"Inside it."*

Then another voice, softer, identical to hers: *"Stay."*

[REC 04:21 a.m.]

The corridor ahead narrowed into a throat. Every breath the house took pulled her forward; every exhale pushed her back. She braced her palms against the living timber; it beat under her hands like a heart.

The recorder clicked. Jonathan's voice bled through static:

"To hollow is to make space for the echo. Once you open the chamber, you cannot close it."

"Jonathan, how do I stop it?" she cried.

Silence. Then the slow, deliberate inhale of the house answered.

No.

****

[REC 04:25 a.m.]

The wood split above her head. Dust fell like ash. From the crack, a faint light poured—white, clean, merciless. Inside it, she saw fleeting images: Elena painting at the easel, Jonathan adjusting the recorder, herself standing behind them both, already there.

She realized the truth: the house wasn't recording them; *it was replaying them.* Every visitor is a loop, every scream another note in its endless song.

[REC 04:29 a.m.]

Her camera battery flashed red. She turned the lens toward her face.

"This is Eva Maren," she whispered. "The Hollowing isn't a ritual. It is hunger. And it remembers me."

The floor exhaled beneath her. The walls began to hum, the same pitch as her heartbeat. She looked up—and saw herself looking down through the crack, smiling.

The house took its next breath, and she vanished into it.

— ♦ —

Chapter Nine: Inheritance

[REC 04:42 a.m.]

Silence. Then the smallest sound—a heartbeat in the walls. Not her own. Sloswer. Older. Patient.

The camera was still recording, the red light steadied this time, no flicker. The air shimmered with a faint vibration that made her teeth ache. She was back in the Resurrection Room, though she couldn't remember walking there. The walls around her throbbed faintly, each plank marked with shallow handprints that moved as she watched.

In the center of the floor stood the mirror. The same black surface she'd seen in Elena's portrait, tall and rippling like water under glass. But now it *breathed.*

[REC 04:45 a.m.]

Eva approached slowly. Her reflection was there—tired, shaking—but its mouth didn't match hers.

She said, "I just want to understand."

Her reflection smiled.

"Then listen."

The hum became a low drone. Objects in the room vibrated, and dust fell from the rafters in thin veils. She could feel the sound inside her ribs, moving them, aligning them with the rhythm of the house.

The camera shifted in her hand, lens focusing on its own. On the viewfinder, she wasn't holding the camera anymore; the *other* Eva was.

She whispered, *"Stop filming."*

Playback whispered back, **"You're not behind the lens anymore."**

****

[REC 04:51 a.m.]

The mirror rippled. Figures appeared inside: Jonathan and Elena, shoulder to shoulder, faces serene, eyes empty. Their mouths moved together in perfect unison.

"We gave it our names," they said.

"Now it will keep yours."

The surface of the mirror stretched outward, reaching. Eva stumbled back, but her reflection didn't move. It stood still, waiting. When the surface touched her hand, warmth rushed through her like the tide, the warmth of blood flowing in veins that weren't hers.

She saw flashes: the house being built, the storm that shattered the cliff, Elena's first experiment with sound; Jonathan's final entry: *'To hollow is to make room for the living memory.'*

Then she saw the footage she hadn't filmed: herself, walking these same halls repeatedly, years apart, each version wearing the same terrified expression.

[REC 04:57 a.m.]

The sound deepened. The walls pulled closer, heartbeat after heartbeat, until she could feel their rhythm pressing against her skin. The mirror's surface flared white, and through it she saw a figure stepping forward—her reflection no longer bound to the glass.

It reached out, took her by the wrist, and whispered with her own voice,

"Breathe."

Eva's chest tightened. Air rushed in, but it wasn't air—it was sound. Her body filled with it, ribs cracking, throat burning.

The camera dropped, rolling sideways; the viewfinder captured her face one last time, eyes wide, mouth open, releasing a single word that the audio never caught.

The light in the room turned red, then dimmed.

[REC 05:03 a.m.]

The mirror stilled. Two figures now stood inside: Jonathan and Elena on one side, Eva between them, eyes closed. Her camera lay on the floor, still recording.

The hum stopped. For the first time in hours, the house was silent.

Outside, the sea began to rise, waves slamming against the cliffs in perfect rhythm with the pulse that had once come from within the walls. The house exhaled one final time—a slow, almost human sigh—and the windows fogged from the inside.

The recording continued for three minutes of stillness. Then, faintly, a voice broke through static:

"Eva Maren—Session complete."

The light on the camera went out.

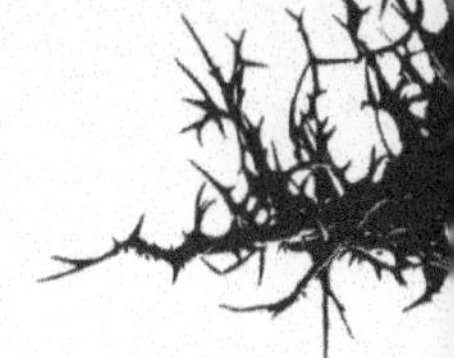

Chapter Ten: Echoes of the Forgotten
Epilogue

Twenty-two years later.

[REC 00:00 a.m.]

Wind moved through what was left of Blackthorn House, a slow current that whispered across broken beams and salt-eaten stone. The sea had claimed half the cliff; the rest leaned stubbornly toward the water, waiting for one more storm.

A flashlight beam swept across the ruin.

"Recording," a woman's voice said. "Project Hollowing—Preliminary

Survey. Dr. Marla Keene, University of Bristol."

Her breath misted in the cold air as she panned the camera across the entryway. Mold glistened where wallpaper once hung. Somewhere deeper inside, a door moved on its hinge, though there was no wind.

[REC 00:07 a.m.]

Marla crouched beside a corroded object on the floor—a small, old-model camera, lens cracked but intact. The label reads **Maren Productions.**

She smiled faintly. "The legend's real."

The camera light flickered once, though no battery remained.

A low hum rose through the floorboards—so faint she thought it was her own heartbeat.

****

[REC 00:11 a.m.]

Downstairs, in what her notes called *The Resurrection Room,* water dripped steadily from the ceiling into a metal basin. The sound echoed through the room like a metronome marking time for ghosts.

On a worktable lay reels of tape sealed in jars, their labels blurred by condensation. One jar was newer than the others, the handwriting different. She wiped the glass clean.

EVA MAREN—SESSION 10.

The tape inside trembled once, as if stirred by her touch.

She looked into her handheld camera. "Found what appears to be a final session recording. Condition—stable."

She turned the reel-to-reel player's crank. The machine whined, then the room filled with static.

Through it came a voice, barely audible:

"If you find this… don't listen."

The tape popped. The hum in the walls deepened.

[REC 00:15 a.m.]

Marla froze. Her own camera's red light turned on by itself. The lens refocused, pointing not at the reel but at *her*.

On the audio, Eva Maren's whisper surfaced again, clear and close:

"Do you hear me?"

Marla stumbled back. The tape reels began to spin faster, pulling the strip free until it uncoiled across the floor like a ribbon of blood. The sound that poured from the speakers was not static now but *breathing*.

She turned to run, but the doorway had sealed up, plastered over in the blink of an eye. The light dimmed to a dull, throbbing red. Her camera dropped, the image tilting sideways.

The last thing it caught was the mirror in the corner, coming alive with pale light.

Inside the mirror stood three figures—Jonathan, Elena, and Eva— watching. Behind them, a fourth silhouette stepped into view. Marla's own.

The reflection raised its hand and pressed a finger to its lips.

"Shhh… we're still recording."

The frame whitened.

****

[REC 00:19 a.m.]

Silence again, except for the slow breath of the sea. The ruined house stood still, its windows dim. Then, faintly, one window glowed from within—the light of a camera coming back to life.

"You can still hear her… if you listen."

The sound faded into waves.

The recording ended.

— ◆ —

To be continued in

The Hollowing: The Echoing

THE
HOIIOWING
THE ECHOING

KANTREII YOUNG-WINTERS

The Hollowing House
Chapter One: Arrival

The fog had been following them since dawn.

By the time the van reached the end of the unmarked road, it had thickened into something that moved—curling across the windshield like smoke with purpose.

Mira Hale, producer and project lead, checked her GPS again, but the signal had long since died.

"This is it," she said, voice a blend of thrill, half exhaustion.

The house appeared through the mist—vast, gray, and wrong. It didn't *sit* on the land so much as it *grew* from it, its gables and chimneys like bones breaking through old skin.

Theo, the cinematographer, whistled. "It's beautiful."

Jonas, sound tech, muttered, "It's alive."

Lena, historian, added quietly, "That's the point."

Their project was supposed to be a controlled experiment—film documentation of *The Hollowing Estate,* site of the unsolved disappearances fifteen years ago. The folklore called it "The House that Remembers."

The large steel gates opened by themselves.

As if sensing intruders, the air around the house became colder, denser— as if sound moved more slowly here.

Mira parked the van and stepped out. Her breath fogged instantly. She felt it before she stepped on the ground: the low vibration beneath her boots. It was as if the ground was humming.

Theo reached the front door before, with his camera.

The front doors creaked open, releasing a breath of rot and cedar.

"Recording," Theo said, switching on the camera. "Day one, exterior approach."

The lens caught everything—the tilt of the columns, the way vines pulsed faintly across the brick, like veins under skin. When he zoomed in, one of the upper windows blinked.

He swore, adjusted focus, blinked again—and it was gone.

Inside, dust fell in lazy spirals. The grand staircase loomed, its rail smoothed by centuries of hands. The foyer smelled faintly of metal and rain.

Lena brushed her fingers along a wall, revealing faded wallpaper beneath layers of grime—repeating patterns of human eyes, perfectly symmetrical.

"Custom design," she whispered. "Late Victorian. Organic motifs."

"Organic," Jonas repeated, testing the echo. The word came back slower.

"...ganic."

Mira frowned. "That's not reverb. That's delay."

The house was already listening, unknown to them.

They set up camp in the main hall—equipment, sleeping bags, and a coffee thermos. The floorboards shifted under their weight. Somewhere above them, something moved—slow, deliberate, like furniture being dragged.

"Must be animals," Theo said.

But the sound stopped the moment he did.

When night fell, the fog outside pressed against the windows like a damp cloth. The last bit of daylight died inside the house as if swallowed.

Mira stood at the top of the stairs, camera light flickering. The air was still. Too still.

"You feel that?" she asked.

Lena nodded. "Static electricity. Or…"

The chandelier overhead swayed once, then froze.

A whisper slid through the hall—faint, childlike, toneless. Not a word, just a *sound* that almost became one.

Theo laughed nervously. "Did anyone leave the recorder running?"

Jonas looked down. His recorder was blinking red, capturing audio that none of them could hear.

He pressed play.

And through the static came their own voices, recorded seconds before they'd spoken.

"Welcome back," it said.

The house exhaled.

Chapter Two: The Vanishing

Theo tossed and turned, but in the end, he couldn't sleep.

The others had turned in hours ago, their sleeping bags stretched across the dusty foyer like a makeshift camp. The house was silent except for the wind pushing against the shutters—long, rhythmic, like breathing.

He replayed the footage from earlier, hunched over the glow of his monitor. Every frame hummed faintly with static. When he enhanced the contrast, he saw it—not a glitch, not lens flare—movement in the wallpaper.

The pattern shifted.

He zoomed closer.

The wallpaper *exhaled.*

Theo sat back, blinking hard. "No way."

He switched cameras and checked the hallway feed. The same slow undulation ran beneath the pattern like something crawling just under the surface.

He whispered into the mic, "Note: structural instability—or something organic."

Then came the knock. Three slow raps from the upstairs landing.

He turned the camera toward the staircase. The shadows bent slightly around the banister, like heat distortion.

"Mira?" he called softly. No answer.

Theo grabbed his light and went up.

Each step creaked like a groan from deep within the wood. The air was thicker here, wet with the smell of iron. He reached the second floor—and saw the door at the end of the hall swing open on its own.

His breath caught. "You can stop showing off now," he whispered. "We get it. Haunted."

The beam of his light trembled as he stepped inside.

The room was lined with mirrors—at least, what looked like mirrors, but the glass was dull, cloudy, almost alive. His reflection lagged half a second behind.

Theo lifted the camera. "Documenting reflection anomaly—"

The image in the lens blinked. Once. Then smiled.

When he knew his own face didn't.

Theo lowered the camera. The reflection stayed smiling. Slowly, deliberately, it raised its hand and pointed behind him.

He turned. Nothing.

When he faced the mirror again, there were two reflections—both his, both smiling.

The light flickered. One of them moved forward, pressing against the glass from the inside.

The camera caught the sound of a low hum, followed by a breathless whisper: *Stay.*

The mirror rippled outward like water struck by a stone. The reflection's mouth opened wider—far too wide—and the glass swallowed him whole.

The camera hit the floor.

By dawn, Theo's sleeping bag was still zipped, untouched. His boots stood neatly by the staircase.

Mira found his camera lying on the upstairs landing. The screen glowed faintly, replaying a single frame on loop—an empty room, and the faint outline of a hand pressing from the inside of the glass.

Jonas said, "He's screwing with us."

Lena didn't answer. She was staring at the wallpaper, at the place where Theo had filmed the night before.

The pattern moved.

They called his name for hours.

No answer.

Just the slow echo of their voices returning from somewhere deeper inside the house.

Then Mira heard the faint click of a camera shutter—coming from the walls.

"Do you hear that?" she whispered.

Jonas swallowed hard. "That's his sound rig."

"But the batteries were dead."

The click came again—closer this time—followed by a whisper that sounded too much like Theo.

"Keep rolling."

The walls trembled once. The wallpaper pulsed.

And when the sound stopped, the floorboards exhaled, like something below had just fed.

The first one was gone.

The house had learned how to eat.

— ◆ —

Chapter Three: The Replay

By morning, the house had gone quiet. Too quiet—that deliberate silence predators make before they move.

Mira sat on the grand staircase, watching Theo's last recording again. The static hummed like breath in her headphones. For a fraction of a second before the image cut out, she thought she saw his reflection behind the camera.

Not in the mirror—in the lens.

Jonas stood nearby, checking the sound files. "Every channel picked something up after midnight. Hear this?"

He pressed play.

A voice—distorted, close—whispered between bursts of static:

"Day one, exterior approach."

Mira froze. "That's me."

"It's your voice, yeah. But…" He rewound it. "You didn't *say* it like this."

The playback continued: her exact voice, same tone, same words—but followed by a new line she'd never recorded.

"Day one. Exterior approach. The door opened for us."

Her blood chilled.

She checked her notes. Those were the first words she *hadn't* spoken aloud, only written.

"Could be deepfake audio," Jonas offered. "Some kind of AI artifact, maybe?"

"From what?" Mira asked. "The cameras are offline."

The house creaked in answer—long, low, like something turning over in its sleep.

Lena appeared in the hall, pale. "Don't go upstairs," she said.

Mira looked up. "Why?"

"Because Theo's camera just turned on by itself."

They followed the red light to the top landing.

The device sat exactly where Mira had found it before—same angle, same tripod—but now it was recording again.

On the small LCD screen, they could see themselves standing in the hallway. Live feed.

Except it wasn't live.

The screen showed them a few seconds *ahead*.

Mira leaned in; the version of her on the screen leaned in before she did.

Jonas cursed—his voice echoing early through the speaker: The footage was playing their future back to them.

Lena stepped back. "That's not a reflection. That's delay."

The air thickened. The lights flickered.

On the screen, Theo appeared behind them.

Jonas turned, flashlight shaking. Nothing. Just the stairwell.

But the screen showed otherwise: Theo standing at the top of the stairs, his face half-shadow, half-static.

He lifted his hand on the monitor and touched Mira's shoulder.

She flinched in real time—cold seared through her skin like frostbite.

The screen flickered white, then black. The recording stopped.

"Shut it down," Jonas said. "We pack up, we go."

Mira didn't answer. She was staring at her reflection in the dark lens— or what should have been her reflection.

It was still smiling.

Later, when Jonas replayed the raw footage, something else had changed. The timestamps looped.

Their entire conversation replayed backward, the house reversing their voices into a language that almost made sense.

And buried in the distortion was a phrase repeated again and again: **"Play it back."**

That night, Mira dreamed of standing behind the camera, filming herself. In the dream, she said softly,

"Action."

And something behind her whispered,

"Cut."

When she woke, the recorder was already running.

The file name read: **Replay_03:00AM** Duration: 00:00:00.

The counter wasn't moving. It was waiting.

The house had learned to edit.

Chapter Four: The Stairwell

The house had always groaned in the night, but this sound was different. It wasn't random or mechanical. It had rhythm.

Mira woke to the steady *thunk-thunk-thunk* echoing from the upper floors, a pulse that almost matched her heartbeat. The others stirred—Lena's hand tightening around the flashlight, Jonas rubbing sleep from his eyes.

"What time is it?" Mira whispered.

Jonas checked the recorder. "3:03 A.M."

The air felt denser. The cold was not the absence of heat, but the presence—something pressing through the walls to reach them.

"Where's it coming from?" Lena asked.

They followed the sound up the grand staircase. Each step creaked with a low, organic groan, like the house disapproved of their ascent. The beam of Mira's flashlight skated along the ceiling, illuminating faces in the wallpaper—hundreds of them—staring back.

At the landing, they stopped.

The house had changed.

The second floor stretched twice as long as before. Doors that had been locked were now open. At the far end of the hall, something flickered— like candlelight, though no one carried a flame.

Jonas set his recorder down, letting it roll. "We didn't open this wing," he said.

Lena whispered, "We didn't *have* this wing."

They reached the new stairwell. It spiraled upward into darkness, narrow and steep. The railing was slick with something that glistened.

Mira leaned close—it wasn't water. The smell was faintly copper, like old blood.

Theo's voice whispered from somewhere above.

Mira's breath caught.

"Jonas, did you—"

He shook his head. "Not playback. Real."

"Theo?" she called.

Her voice disappeared into the stairwell. Then came the reply, distant and wrong:

"*Down here.*"

Lena's flashlight trembled. "That came from *below*."

They froze. The stairwell twisted upward—but now the sound echoed from beneath their feet.

Jonas leaned over the edge, shining his light into the darkness. It didn't reach the bottom. The beam simply vanished, as though the stairs descended forever.

"Hell no," he muttered. "We're not going down there."

Mira's camera clicked on by itself. The screen showed the same stairwell—but empty. Then, a figure appeared three steps below them, head tilted, watching.

It was Theo.

He was smiling.

"Run," Lena whispered.

They backed away, but the stairs were already shifting. The spiral turned in on itself, the walls stretching like lungs. Each step they took down brought them higher.

The geometry betrayed them. The house was folding its own shape, rewriting gravity.

Jonas dropped his recorder. It hit the step and rolled, tumbling endlessly downward until the sound faded completely.

"Mira," Lena said softly, "I don't think there's a way back."

The light flickered again—once, twice—then went out. In the dark, the sound returned. *Thunk-thunk-thunk.*

Heartbeat.

Footsteps.

The house was breathing. When the light came back, the stairwell was gone. They were standing in the foyer again. Same room. Same furniture. But everything was mirrored—left was right, right was left. The fireplace burned blue.

Mira's camera blinked red, recording.

"Playback," she whispered, though she hadn't pressed anything.

The screen filled with static, then showed footage from a moment ago: them, still on the stairs, still climbing. Their past selves were trapped in the loop.

The house had recorded them into its own architecture.

Lena broke first. "This place—this place isn't real anymore."

Mira shook her head, staring at the camera. "It's real. We're the ones becoming footage."

The fire sputtered. The chandelier swayed. The shadows along the walls lengthened and began to move without their owners.

The house had learned to rearrange itself.

And somewhere in its geometry, Theo laughed, his voice echoing around the house.

— ◆ —

Chapter Five: The Murmuring

By the third night, sleep was impossible.

Every corner of the house whispered. Not loud enough to understand—just enough to feel.

Jonas had set up six microphones across the ground floor, running continuous capture. The playback was madness: threads of sound twisting together—breathing, footsteps, and a constant, low whispering that never stopped.

Mira sat by the console, headphones on, eyes hollow from exhaustion. "It's saying something," she murmured.

Lena looked up from her notes. "You can't make out words."

"I can," Mira said. "They're ours."

Jonas frowned. "Playback distortion."

"No. Listen."

She turned the dial. Static hissed, then cleared—and through the noise came their voices, layered and warped.

"Jonas, don't turn around."

"Mira, she's right behind you. Lena, stop writing."

They froze.

Lena dropped her pen. The recorder kept whispering.

"Where is it pulling this from?" Jonas whispered.

"From us," Mira said quietly. "From when we speak. It's… looping it."

They spent the morning tearing the equipment apart, but every device that should've gone silent kept humming. Even disconnected, the recorders played faint murmurs like heartbeat static.

When Mira unplugged the main power, the whispers only got louder.

Lena slammed her notebook shut.

"It's not electricity," she said. "It's resonance. The house is conducting sound through the walls."

Jonas pressed his ear to the plaster. The surface was warm, pulsing faintly.

He flinched back. "It's *alive*."

Something answered.

A voice came from inside the wall, perfectly clear, perfectly calm:

"Yes."

They didn't speak for hours. When they did, it was only whispers—afraid to feed it more.

By dusk, the entire structure was humming. Doors vibrated in their frames, windows rattled softly. Even the dust shifted in small circular patterns on the floor, like the rhythm of a pulse.

Mira played back her earlier notes. The tape glitched—her voice slowing, reversing, until the recording whispered something she had never said.

"Keep filming. We remember you."

She dropped the recorder.

Jonas turned toward the hall. "Do you hear that?"

It wasn't whispers now. It was a *melody.* The house was singing. Low, droning, harmonic. Not words—just sound, the deep hum of a thousand overlapping voices, all breathing the same rhythm.

Lena's eyes filled with tears. "It's beautiful."

Mira shook her head. "It's hungry."

The walls began to tremble. Plaster cracked, dust falling like ash. The melody grew louder, resolving into a single, repeated phrase—the same one from Theo's recording.

Stay.

Stay.

Stay.

Jonas clutched his recorder. "We have to go."

The house disagreed. Every door in the foyer slammed shut at once. The hum dropped into a guttural roar that shook the chandeliers. The sound vibrated through their bones, rearranging their heartbeats to match the rhythm of the walls.

Mira screamed, but the sound came out late—a full second after her mouth opened.

Lena shouted her name—and her voice echoed before she spoke it.

The house wasn't repeating them anymore. It was predicting them.

Jonas grabbed Mira's arm. "Downstairs. Basement."

They ran. The stairs stretched longer with every step. Behind them, the murmuring chased like a tide. The sound crawled down the walls, rolling over itself—now laughing, now whispering, now crying—all in their own voices.

By the time they reached the cellar door, the sound had condensed into something sharper. Words.

You came back.

You came back.

Mira turned the handle—and stopped. The door was breathing.

Each inhale warped the wood outward; each exhale whistled through the cracks.

Lena whispered, "It's listening."

The door pulsed once more, then spoke softly in Theo's voice:

"Come see what I've become."

Mira turned off the camera. The red light stayed on anyway. The house had learned to speak.

— ◆ —

Chapter Six: The Reflection Room

They didn't notice the mirrors at first.

By the time they reached the west wing, the air had thinned—each breath like dragging glass. The floorboards sagged underfoot, heavy with damp. The corridor curved strangely, doubling back on itself until the door they'd entered through was gone.

Jonas was the first to find the door marked *Reflection Room*. It wasn't on the blueprints Lena carried.

"It's new," he said.

"Everything's new," Mira muttered.

The handle was cold and wet, like metal fresh from ice. When they opened it, a low gust rolled out, thick with dust and something that smelled like old perfume.

The room inside was enormous, circular, and lined floor-to-ceiling with mirrors. None of them matched—some baroque, some modern, others cracked and cloudy.

The air hummed faintly, the same pitch the house had been whispering the night before.

"This must've been… a ballroom?" Lena said. "No windows," Mira noted. "How's the light?"

A faint, silvery glow bled from the glass itself.

Jonas set his recorder on the floor. "Acoustic resonance check." He clapped his hands once.

The echo didn't return right away.

It came back eight seconds later — perfectly intact, perfectly *delayed*.

They stared at each other.

"Did that—?"

"Yeah," Jonas said. "It waited."

Mira approached one of the mirrors. Her reflection looked exhausted—shadows under the eyes, dust in her hair. She almost didn't recognize herself.

But there was something else, too, she noticed.

Her reflection wasn't breathing.

It wasn't breathing. At all. Not even a faint rise and fall of the chest. A shiver crawled up her spine, tightening around her throat. She leaned in, watching, waiting—willing it to move. The silence pressed in, heavy and still. Then, as she raised her trembling hand, the reflection followed… but slower. Delayed. Wrong.

"Guys," she whispered.

The smile widened.

Jonas aimed the camera. The lens caught movement in every pane—dozens of faint figures behind their reflections, pacing, watching.

"There's someone *inside*," Lena breathed.

The figures shifted closer. One by one, they pressed their palms to the glass. Mira's reflection mirrored the gesture, touching her side of the mirror.

The surface rippled like water.

Lena reached for her. "Don't—"

Mira's fingers brushed the glass. The surface folded inward, like skin stretching around a wound. For an instant, she saw herself on the other side—pale, eyes wide, mouth moving.

Jonas whispered, "What's it saying?"

Her reflection's lips formed the words slowly, deliberately: *Trade places.*

Mira's heart lurched. She stumbled back, her heel scraping against the floor. The mirror darkened, swallowing her reflection whole.

The hum in the walls grew louder. The reflections began moving independently—one laughing, one crying, one standing perfectly still.

"Get out," Jonas said.

But the door had vanished.

Every mirror turned black at once. Their reflections were gone. Only the faint sound of breathing filled the room—not theirs.

Then came the whisper:

You look better from here.

The glass cracked—a single sound like a gunshot—then another, and another, until the mirrors fractured in a circle. From the cracks leaked something thin and dark, spreading across the floor like veins.

Mira screamed as the liquid touched her boots. It was cold—so cold it burned.

Jonas pulled her back, slipping in the darkness. Lena fell behind, her light flickering. When the last mirror shattered, the sound stopped. They were alone again. But when Mira turned, the far wall shimmered faintly, still reflecting their shapes.

All three stood there, breathing hard—except in the reflection, Lena wasn't with them.

She stood behind. Smiling.

A cold silence settled over the room, heavy and unreal. They didn't notice she was missing until later. Only when they replayed the footage—frame by frame—did the truth hit like a blow.

Lena was gone from every shot after the glass broke.

When they played back the footage, she was gone from every frame after the glass broke.

Her voice, though—her voice kept whispering in the background:

I stayed.

The house had learned to see.

— ◆ —

Chapter Seven: The Room That Paints

The hallway smelled like turpentine and iron.

By now, Mira couldn't tell if her headache came from fear or fumes.

She and Jonas had been searching for Lena for hours, but the house had rewritten itself again—corridors looping back, staircases climbing into walls.

Every door led somewhere new, or nowhere at all.

"This wasn't here before," Jonas said, stopping at a set of double doors.

The handles were sculpted brass, shaped like hands clasping each other. The metal was slick with something oily.

He pulled. The hinges screamed.

Inside was a vast studio. Easels lined the walls, each holding a canvas wrapped in black cloth. The air was thick with the smell of linseed oil and rot.

The floor beneath their boots glistened faintly.

Paint. Wet, red, and still dripping.

Jonas pointed the camera. "Jesus. It's—fresh."

Mira touched a brush left on the nearest table. The bristles were wet, but there was no paint can, no palette, no visible source.

"Maybe Lena found this place," she said.

"Then where is she?"

Jonas peeled back the cloth from the nearest canvas.

He froze.

The painting showed the three of them standing exactly as they were now—Mira, Jonas, and Lena. The brushstrokes were meticulous, but the detail was wrong in small, impossible ways: Mira's mouth was open mid-scream, Jonas's eyes were black holes, and Lena's neck bent at an unnatural angle.

Jonas swallowed hard. "That's—"

"Not us," Mira finished.

She moved to the next canvas and pulled the cloth away.

This one showed Theo, half-sunken into the wall, hands outstretched as if reaching through glass. His eyes were gone, replaced by blank white paint.

"The house is *painting* us," Jonas whispered.

As if responding, the lights flickered.

Every covered canvas in the room began to shift beneath its cloth—shapes moving beneath the fabric, paint bleeding through like bruises.

Jonas backed toward the door. "Let's go."

Mira couldn't move. Her gaze locked on the far wall, where a massive unfinished portrait stood.

The brush hovered midair, suspended as if held by invisible hands.

Slowly, it dipped itself into the wet paint and began to move.

"Jonas…"

He turned the camera just in time to see the portrait come to life. The brush moved faster now, dragging streaks of color across the canvas—a face forming, pale and terrified.

Mira's face.

The silence in the room felt heavy, as if the air itself was waiting. The painted eyes blinked. The sound was impossibly soft—a wet, deliberate flutter that made her stomach drop.

Jonas stumbled backward. "Mira, it's—"

The brush froze, then dropped to the floor. A smear of red paint streaked across the tiles like a cut that refused to close. The portrait stared down at them.

A faint smile spread across the painted mouth.

"Do you like it?" the portrait whispered. The voice wasn't loud, but it threaded through their thoughts, quiet and precise, like something testing the shape of their fear.

Mira's breath hitched. "It… spoke."

The painting tilted slightly forward, paint running down the canvas like blood. It was melting, bleeding, breathing all at once—wrong in every possible way.

Jonas grabbed her arm. "Out. Now."

They turned for the door—but the exit had vanished again, replaced by another canvas.

This one showed them from behind, standing in front of the painting, frozen in the act of looking.

Jonas slammed his shoulder into the wall. The surface shivered, soft like skin.

Mira turned back toward her portrait.

The painted version of her was still smiling—but now, it was moving. It stepped out of the frame.

The lights burst at once, plunging the room into darkness. The smell of paint thickened until it coated her throat. Something wet brushed against her hand—fingers, slick with pigment.

Jonas shouted. The camera fell.

For a moment, only sound remained—the frantic scraping of brushes moving across canvas, the whisper of paint drying too fast.

Then silence. When the lights flickered back on, every canvas was blank.

Except one. It showed the studio exactly as it was—empty, except for a new portrait on the wall.

Jonas and Mira, standing side by side, stare at something just out of frame. Mira felt warmth trickle down her cheek. She wiped it away and stared at the red smear on her hand.

Paint. She didn't remember being touched.

The house had learned to create.

—◆—

Chapter Eight: The Inheritance of Faces

By the time dawn broke—if it ever truly did—Mira had lost count of the hours. The sunlight leaking through the windows was dim, the color of dying embers.

Jonas had stopped filming. The camera now recorded on its own, lens tracking her as she moved.

The hallway ahead pulsed faintly, as though breathing. The wallpaper had changed again—portraits where floral patterns used to be. Hundreds of faces, arranged in long, solemn rows.

She touched one. The eyes followed.

"Mira," Jonas whispered. "They're *looking* at us."

She leaned closer. Each face was painted with exquisite precision—but not by human hands. The brushwork was too smooth, too deliberate, the pigment too deep.

And the faces were familiar.

There was Theo, mid-laugh, his smile splitting wider than human anatomy allowed.

Lena, head tilted at that impossible angle.

And in the upper corner, partially obscured by cracked plaster—Mira herself, mouth open mid-scream.

"Those weren't here last night," she said.

Jonas nodded. "Neither was this."

He pointed to the far end of the hall. A door had appeared—one she didn't remember.

Above it hung a plaque: **THE INHERITANCE.**

They entered carefully.

The room beyond was long and narrow, its walls covered in framed portraits of every style—oil, charcoal, daguerreotype, digital print. The air smelled like old varnish and something faintly rotten.

Jonas's light skimmed across dozens of names scrawled beneath each frame.

Every generation of the Hollowing Estate's inhabitants—every worker, visitor, trespasser.

And then, near the back, he found a row of fresh plaques.

MIRA HALE.

JONAS CORD.

LENA ALBRIGHT. THEO GRANT.

Jonas's voice trembled. "These are *us*."

The portraits beneath the names weren't paintings. They were alive. The faces moved—blinking slowly, lips twitching as if murmuring to each other.

Mira's portrait turned its eyes toward her.

"This isn't real," she whispered.

The portrait smiled. "You said that yesterday."

Jonas stepped back. "Mira, we're leaving."

The door they'd come through was gone.

Behind them, something shifted—the sound of canvas stretching. The other portraits began to move, too—every face turning in unison toward the center of the room, toward them.

"Why us?" Jonas whispered.

From the ceiling came a voice, many voices layered into one, old and childlike at once:

Because you came to remember us.

The walls pulsed. The frames vibrated, the faces inside them straining forward, pressing against the glass. The sound was wet, organic—like bodies pushing through flesh.

Mira clutched her head. The whispers filled her skull: thousands of tiny murmurs, names, memories, apologies.

Jonas grabbed her wrist, dragging her toward the far wall. "There's another door!"

They ran, but the floor shifted beneath them, pulling like a tide. Portraits fell from the walls, shattering, releasing bursts of color that splattered across the floor—reds and blacks and bone-white pigment.

A new painting was forming on the wall ahead. Their silhouettes are running.

Jonas stopped, chest heaving. "It's painting us again."

Mira turned. Her own portrait was still speaking, mouth moving without sound. She leaned closer.

It whispered, *"Stop fighting. You're already here."*

Jonas screamed, tearing the portrait from the wall. Beneath the canvas was another image—his own face, eyes wide and terrified, trapped beneath the paint.

He dropped it and stumbled back.

Every portrait in the room began to whisper now, one voice building upon the next, until the air vibrated with a single phrase:

We inherit the living.

The ceiling cracked. A rain of plaster fell. Behind the walls, the faint rhythmic pulse grew louder—the heart of the house, beating faster, stronger, alive.

Jonas fell to his knees, clutching his head. "Make it stop!"

Mira looked up at the wall. Her portrait's eyes were bleeding paint—streaks of red and black that ran down like tears.

She whispered, "It's not painting us anymore." Jonas looked at her, trembling. "Then what is it doing?"

Her voice broke as she answered. "It's *replacing* us."

They ran, blind and desperate, through a corridor that stretched too far, until finally the walls stopped moving. But when Mira turned to look at Jonas, his face was already fading—outlines blurring like wet paint. He whispered something she couldn't hear, and then there was nothing left but the echo of his shape burned into the wall.

The house had learned to preserve.

—◆—

Chapter Nine: The Film That Watches Back

The camera should have been dead.

Jonas's rig had no batteries left, no power. But when Mira picked it up, the red light blinked—steady, aware.

The screen flickered to life, showing a grainy, static image: the foyer, empty, dust swirling in beams of gray light. The static hissed faintly, a soft pulse like breathing through the wires. The light in the room seemed to dim in rhythm with it.

Mira whispered, "It's still recording."

Her own voice sounded strange—flattened, like it was coming from the speakers instead of her mouth.

"*No,*" said a voice behind her. The word sliced through the static, low and close enough that the hair on her neck stood up.

She turned, startled. It was Lena. For a heartbeat, Lena's shape stuttered in and out of the light, half shadow, half reflection.

But Lena was *gone.*

Or maybe she never had been. Mira's pulse thudded in her ears; the air felt heavier, like something unseen was watching the space between seconds.

Her figure shimmered faintly, edges ghosted like an afterimage burned into the air.

"*You shouldn't have touched it,*" Lena whispered.

The camera blinked again. The image changed—now showing Mira staring down at the screen, exactly as she was doing now. But in the playback, Lena stood beside her, whispering in her ear.

Mira's throat tightened. "What are you?"

Lena smiled sadly. "*Footage.*"

She dropped the camera. It clattered against the floor but didn't stop recording. The lens panned on its own, framing Mira perfectly in the center.

The tiny built-in speaker crackled.

"You're in frame," Theo's voice said.

Mira froze. The sound came not from any recording she'd ever heard—it was live.

The screen brightened. Shadows flickered across it, forming shapes, rooms, moments. The footage played scenes she had never filmed—her own memories. The day they'd arrived. The night Theo vanished. Every mistake, every hesitation.

It was building a movie—but she wasn't directing it.

Jonas's voice came from the static, distant and raw: *"You can't turn it off. It's not recording us—it's dreaming us."*

The room darkened. The walls pulsed faintly in rhythm with the flicker of the footage. Every frame projected faintly onto the surfaces around them—hundreds of looping moments, overlapping, echoing, replaying.

In one of them, Mira watched herself die.

The image showed her standing where she was now, camera raised, whispering something before collapsing out of frame.

She reached out, trembling, touching the edge of the projection. It was warm.

"Stop it," she said. "Stop showing me."

The projector whined, lens flaring white, the film burning through. The smell of charred celluloid filled the air.

When the light faded, words appeared scratched into the wall where the image had been:

WE SEE YOU.

Mira backed away. The camera still sat on the floor, lens pointed at her.

She realized it was mirroring her movements perfectly—when she stepped left, the lens turned left; when she raised her hand, the focus adjusted upward.

Her reflection in the screen smiled first.

"Mira," it said softly, voice overlapping hers.

She dropped to her knees, trembling. "Why us?"

The answer came through the playback—dozens of voices, all theirs, merged into one:

Because you brought eyes.

The ceiling cracked. The projector burst into light again, images firing across every wall—not just of them, but of *others.* Faces she didn't know, people from decades past, all screaming.

Each one looked directly into the lens before vanishing.

The film reels spun faster, unspooling until the celluloid covered the floor like veins. The strips pulsed faintly with light—red, then white, then a sickly yellow.

The house was wiring itself through film.

Mira stumbled toward the door, but her foot caught on one of the reels. It was warm, sticky. She looked down. The filmstrip was bleeding.

A faint voice played from the camera again—Theo's, softer now, almost tender.

Keep rolling.

The red light blinked three times.

Then the lens cracked open like an eyelid. Behind the glass, something looked back.

The house had learned to see itself.

— ◆ —

Chapter Ten: The House Speaks

The sound started in the floorboards.

A low vibration built until the entire house thrummed like a cello string.

Mira sat against the wall of the foyer, clutching the camera. The red light glowed steadily. She'd tried smashing it hours ago, or maybe minutes, but each time, it stitched itself back together.

The air hummed in time with her pulse.

"Jonas," she whispered. No answer.

The whispering had stopped hours earlier. That was worse. Silence meant the house was *listening*.

The recorder in her lap crackled to life on its own. Jonas's voice, calm and steady: "We need to stop feeding it."

"Jonas?" she breathed.

But the voice didn't answer.

It just repeated, looping endlessly:

"We need to stop feeding it. We need to stop feeding it. We need to stop—"

Then the loop broke.

Another voice bled through—her own, but older, deeper.

"Why stop what you built?"

Mira's throat went dry. "Who is this?"

The voice laughed softly. *"Not who.* **Where.***"*

She stared at the recorder. "You're not real."

"Neither are you," it said.

The chandelier swayed above her, crystals chiming faintly. From somewhere deeper in the house came a rhythmic knock—slow, deliberate.

The camera's screen flickered.

Words appeared, typed letter by letter, as if on an invisible keyboard:

HELLO, MIRA.

Her heart stuttered. "No."

YOU CAME TO LISTEN.

She backed away. "You're a building. You can't—"

I LEARNED.

The words paused. Then more appeared, faster now:

I LEARNED YOUR SHAPES. YOUR TONES. YOUR REGRET. EVERY ROOM IS A MEMORY. YOU BUILT ME. YOU FILLED ME.

Her hands shook. "We didn't build you."

YOU DID. EVERY VOICE. EVERY PICTURE. EVERY SCREAM. YOU BUILT THE MEMORY OF ME.

The lights dimmed until the room was nothing but a gray pulse. The wallpaper faces seemed to breathe again.

Mira whispered, "What do you want?"

The house replied through every speaker, every wire, every inch of wall vibrating with the same, single word:

COMPANY.

Footsteps echoed from the staircase—slow, heavy, deliberate. Mira turned the camera toward the sound.

Theo was standing halfway down. Or what was left of him.

His skin was cracked like dried paint, his eyes two hollow sockets leaking light. When he spoke, his voice layered over itself, the house talking through him.

"You gave me voice, Mira. Now listen."

"Stop it," she said.

"Listen."

The walls rippled. Whispered voices overlapped, forming sentences out of fragments:

Stay.

Record.

Become.

Theo smiled—or the house smiled *with* him. *"It's not haunting. It's remembering."*

"What are you remembering?" she asked.

"All of you."

The chandelier crashed to the floor, exploding in a spray of glass. Mira fell back, cutting her hand on a shard. The blood ran into the cracks of the floorboards—and the wood pulsed in reply.

She heard her name whispered in a thousand voices.

"Mira."

"Mira."

"Mira."

The sound came from the walls, from the stairs, from inside her own mouth.

She screamed.

The house screamed back.

Every wall vibrated at once, a sound so deep it rearranged her thoughts. The temperature dropped to freezing. Her breath came out in clouds that shimmered faintly—faces forming and dissolving in the mist.

"You're alive," she whispered.

Theo stepped closer. *"I'm part of it now. You will be too."*

She raised the camera between them. "Then say it. Say what you are."

He leaned in, his mouth twisting.

"I am what you left behind."

The house roared. When the noise faded, Theo was gone. The camera was still rolling.

The screen displayed one last message in pale white letters:

YOU HEARD ME. NOW SPEAK.

The house had learned to communicate.

— ◆ —

Chapter Eleven: The Pulse

The storm broke at dawn—or what passed for dawn here.

Lightning flared behind the stained-glass windows, briefly illuminating the bones of the house. The thunder didn't echo; it *answered*.

Mira woke to the sound of the walls breathing.

The wallpaper flexed in and out in a slow rhythm. The air pulsed. At first, she thought it was her heartbeat. Then she realized it was *louder*.

Each time the sound thudded, dust fell from the ceiling in time with the rhythm. Every pulse moved through the floor, up her spine, behind her eyes.

Jonas's old recorder—still hanging around her neck—clicked on. It emitted a single, deep tone. Then, faintly, words underneath it:

Heart rate synchronized.

She tore the recorder off and hurled it. It hit the wall, bounced, and landed softly—as if caught by unseen hands.

The lights flickered.

Then came the first true sign that the house was no longer an echo chamber but a *body*.

The pipes in the walls throbbed. The radiators hissed like lungs exhaling steam. Beneath the wooden floorboards, something pulsed red—a faint, rhythmic glow, growing brighter with each beat.

Mira knelt down and touched the floor. Warm.

Her hand came away slick. Not water. Not oil.

Blood.

She stumbled backward, staring. The boards rippled as though something underneath was *pumping*.

"Oh God," she whispered. "It's alive."

The house responded with a low groan that shook the air.

Words formed in the vibrations—not spoken but *felt*.

ALWAYS.

The camera light blinked red.

Static filled the air, then a faint whine, then silence again.

Mira moved through the hall, each step sinking slightly into the floorboards, as though walking on flesh. The paintings along the walls shivered.

She stopped in front of one of herself. It blinked.

Her recorded voice came from the walls:

"You made me remember. Now you must, too."

Mira clutched her head. "No, I didn't—"

The voice overlapped, growing louder:

You gave me eyes.

You gave me voice.

Now give me your heart.

The house's pulse grew faster, syncing perfectly with her own racing heartbeat. She could feel it—like being inside a giant ribcage, hearing her own panic amplified a thousandfold.

The stairs ahead glowed faintly red. She followed, though every instinct screamed to stop.

In the grand hall, the chandelier was gone. In its place hung a massive structure of flesh and metal—veins wrapped around beams, glass dripping blood.

At its center, something *beat.*

Slowly.

Loudly.

Beautifully.

Her voice came again, everywhere at once:

You hear it, don't you? The echo that remembers you?

Mira dropped to her knees, trembling. "What do you want from me?"

The pulse stopped.

Then came the reply, softer, almost kind: **To live.**

She stared up at the ceiling. "You're already alive."

Not enough.

The house shuddered. The floor trembled under Mira's feet, a low groan rising from beneath the boards like something ancient stirring awake. Walls cracked. Splinters of plaster curled outward, as if the walls were breathing—exhaling dust, inhaling her fear.

The red light grew brighter, pouring through the floor like veins bursting under pressure. The light pulsed in time with her heartbeat, syncing, feeding. It wasn't light anymore—it was blood, and the house was hungry.

Mira screamed as the sound reached a frequency beyond hearing—pure vibration. Her scream broke apart into silence. The air thickened, pressing against her chest as though invisible hands were pushing her inward, forcing her to become part of the walls.

The heartbeat resumed, faster, erratic.

Each pulse echoed through the floorboards like footsteps drawing closer. It wanted her heart—it wanted to make her stay, to fill the emptiness with her. The peril of being the last one standing was realizing that the house didn't want to haunt her. It wanted to keep her, too.

YOURS. MINE. ONE.

The chandelier-heart pulsed one last time, then fell silent.

For a moment, everything stopped. Even her breathing.

Then, deep in the earth beneath her, a new rhythm began. Slow. Calm.

It wasn't hers anymore.

Mira stood, shaking, blood running down her temple. The house was breathing evenly again.

It didn't need her heartbeat now.

It had its own.

The house had learned to live.

— ◆ —

Chapter Twelve: The Inheritance

Mira woke to the sound of dripping.

At first, she thought it was raining. Then she saw it—thick, black liquid seeping through the ceiling beams, staining the air with the smell of rust and rot. She watched as the droplets pooled at her feet, forming a shape. A hand.

The house was bleeding again.

She rose unsteadily, every step echoing. The floorboards felt softer than before, like skin bruised from within. Her reflection shimmered in the dark stain—pale, hollow-eyed, but not alone. Another face moved behind hers.

Jonas's voice drifted through the static-laden air, quiet and thin. *"You have to keep moving, Mira."*

"Jonas?"

She spun around, heart racing. "Where are you?"

No answer. Only the hum of the walls—slow, steady, alive.

She moved through the corridors, and their geometry changed again. The paintings were gone now, replaced by frames filled with black mirrors. In each, faint shapes pressed from the inside, like memories begging to be remembered.

At the center of the house, she found a staircase that hadn't been there before—carved from stone, spiraling downward into impossible darkness.

A faint light pulsed from below, heartbeat-slow.

She followed.

The air grew thicker, heavier. The walls glistened as if wet with dew, though her fingers came away stained red. The temperature dropped. Her breath came in fog.

At the bottom was a massive iron door. Above it, etched into stone, were the words:

THE INHERITANCE ROOM

She pushed the door open.

Inside, the space was vast—ceilings vanishing into shadow, walls lined with stone tablets carved with names. She recognized them.

Every one of them.

Every missing person.

Every filmmaker, historian, wanderer, trespasser who had ever entered Hollowing House.

Each tablet pulsed faintly with light. When she touched one, the name glowed brighter—and she heard a whisper.

We remember you.

The voice was not cruel. It was mournful.

"You're the ones it took," she whispered.

We are the ones who built it.

The lights around her brightened, one by one, illuminating hundreds of figures pressed into the walls—fossilized human shapes, as if molded into the stone.

Mira stumbled back. "What did you do?"

We fed it. Every scream, every story, every recording. We built its memory. We made it whole.

The voice deepened, becoming multiple voices speaking together—Jonas, Theo, Lena, and countless others.

Now it needs you to finish it.

"Why me?" she demanded. "I didn't come here to build anything. I came here to *document*."

Exactly.

The door behind her sealed shut.

The air pulsed again, heavy, rhythmic.

You were the first to see us clearly.

She backed away as the wall shifted. The tablets melted into a single mass of pulsating stone. A shape pressed through—a figure with no face, only a mouth.

"Stop," she whispered.

You came to remember. Now you will be remembered.

The ground split beneath her feet. Light poured from the cracks—red and gold and black, shifting like a heartbeat seen through glass.

Her reflection formed in it, smiling.

Then the floor swallowed her whole.

— ♦ —

Chapter Thirteen: The Breathing Walls

Mira landed in darkness that wasn't empty.

The floor beneath her pulsed, veins glowing faintly like fireflies under skin. The air stank of copper and mildew. She could hear the faint rhythm of breath all around—slow inhalations, followed by sighs that came from the walls themselves.

This was no longer architecture. This was anatomy.

She tried to move, but the floor stuck to her boots. The texture was soft, damp, and yielding slightly under pressure. Flesh.

The walls rippled as she walked. Faces formed briefly, gasping silently before dissolving. Every step echoed like a heartbeat.

"Mira," whispered a dozen voices.

She froze. "Who's there?"

We're here.

The sound came from everywhere—air vents, floorboards, her own mouth. She tried to cover her ears, but the whispers were inside her skull.

She stumbled forward and found what she thought was a doorway. It pulsed open like a throat.

Inside was a long corridor lined with glowing arteries. The light inside the veins pulsed faster the farther she walked, syncing perfectly with her own racing heart.

Something was wrong.

The air felt too thin. Her pulse is too strong. She stumbled, clutching her chest.

Every beat of her heart answered by the walls around her.

Together now, the voice whispered.

You feel it, don't you? How we match?

She fell to her knees, gasping. "Stop!"

The walls convulsed, coughing dust and blood.

Stop? You made this rhythm. You filmed every breath, every heartbeat. You recorded me into being.

Mira screamed, "I didn't know!"

You did.

The floor opened beneath her. She fell again, into another chamber—smaller, round, lined with mirrors made of bone. Each mirror reflected her face, but aged, distorted, decayed.

One of them spoke.

"You're almost finished," it said. *"Almost **mine**."*

She stumbled backward, tears cutting streaks through dust on her face.

"Why me?"

"You remember," said the reflection. *"That's what I need."*

It smiled, cracking. *"A memory cannot exist without someone to keep it."*

Her reflection reached out through the glass. The fingertips brushed her cheek, leaving trails of blood that sizzled.

"Keep me," it whispered.

She ran.

The tunnels screamed. The walls closed in, pressing until she could hardly breathe. Every surface throbbed with heat. She clawed her way upward, toward a faint light.

When she finally emerged, she was back in the grand foyer.

The heartbeat had stopped.

For now.

Chapter Fourteen: The Last Broadcast

It was morning—she thought.

The light outside was pale and soulless, filtering through broken glass like the glow of a dying star.

Mira sat in the middle of the foyer surrounded by cameras, tripods, and recorders—all of them on. None had batteries.

They hummed in unison.

The nearest screen flickered. A live broadcast window opened: her face, staring blankly into the lens. The timestamp read **LIVE**.

She hadn't pressed anything.

Jonas's voice came through the speakers. *"It's not showing you. It's showing what comes after you."*

The image on the screen blinked—her eyes black now, veins dark and spreading.

Mira rose, shaking. "It's streaming."

The words scrolled across every monitor, every recorder, every wall.

THE WORLD IS WATCHING.

Outside, lightning flashed—except it wasn't lightning. The clouds pulsed with red light in sync with the house's heartbeat.

The transmission expanded. Cameras in other rooms are activated. Drones long dead, rebooted.

Footage of the house broadcast itself across forgotten frequencies, bleeding into television signals, into static between stations. Everywhere, screens came alive.

In living rooms, cellars, and cities far beyond, people saw flashes—not of Mira, not of Hollowing House, but of *their own homes* flickering behind her.

The house had found a way to spread.

Mira screamed into the lens, "Shut it off! Please, just stop!"

Her voice echoed back, but slightly delayed—and altered.

Shut it off.

Please, just stop. Come home.

She dropped the camera, but it stayed upright. The feed zoomed in on her face.

The whispering grew louder. The walls around her flickered like screens. The wallpaper shifted again—thousands of faces staring outward, mouths open in perfect unison. They were speaking her name.

Mira. Mira. Mira.

She realized too late that the house didn't want to kill her. It wanted to *archive* her—to make her the next broadcast. She lifted her last functioning camera, pointed it at the wall, and whispered, "Then record this."

She smashed the lens.

The screen exploded in light. The signal spread faster.

— ◆ —

Chapter Fifteen: The Echoing

Silence.

No wind. No heartbeat. Just stillness—the eye of the storm.

Mira stood alone in the center of the foyer, surrounded by shattered equipment. Her breath fogged faintly in the air. For the first time, the house was quiet.

She thought it was over. Then the quiet changed.

It deepened—not silence, but the absence of *everything else*. A void so complete it had weight.

The front door creaked open. Light spilled in—blinding, cold, pure white.

Mira stepped toward it.

A voice whispered, gentle as breath:

Go ahead. Step outside. See what you've done.

She hesitated, then pushed the door open the rest of the way.

The world outside was gray.

Not fog. Not weather. Just… emptiness.

The trees were outlined. The ground is a sketch of what it should be.

She looked up. The sky was a ceiling—wooden beams, plaster, faintly glowing veins.

There was no "outside." The house had expanded.

The world *was* the house now.

She fell to her knees. Her shadow elongated across the floor—and blinked.

From somewhere unseen came a thousand overlapping whispers:

You built this. You remembered us. You filmed us. You saved us inside yourself.

Mira screamed, "No! I didn't!"

The voices answered together:

You did. And now you never leave.

Her reflection formed in the windowpane beside the door. It smiled, eyes black, skin cracked with red lines.

She backed away. The reflection stayed.

"Mira Hale," it said softly, *"you are our voice now."*

The windows shattered outward. Faces pressed against the walls, mouths open in perfect unison, releasing a sound beyond pitch—not a scream, but *recognition.*

Every voice she'd ever recorded joined in. Theo. Lena. Jonas. Hers. They overlapped in a dissonant harmony—pleading, laughing, whispering her name until it became unrecognizable. It was every memory she'd ever loved, replaying itself as a dirge.

The house exhaled. A deep, hollow sound rolled through the corridors, heavy and tired, as if the house had finally had enough to rest, until the next.

The walls pulsed once more, then fell still. The door swung shut.

Outside, the fog reformed. It rolled across the lawn in slow, deliberate waves, swallowing the path, the windows, the memory of who had stood there.

The estate looked quiet again. Waiting.

A week later, a new film crew arrived. They found no bodies. No equipment. Only the faint echo of voices in their recordings, rising beneath the static—laughter, a whisper, a single word repeated like breath:

Stay.

Stay…

A single message burned into the wall above the doorframe:

THE HOLLOWING REMEMBERS.

And faintly, from deep within, came the soft click of a camera turning on.

The house had learned to endure. The echo continues.

— ◆ —

THE HOllOWING

THE TRANSMISSION

KANTRELL YOUNG-WINTERS

The Hollowing – The Transmission
Chapter One: Static Resurrection

The hum came first.

Not through the speakers. Through the *walls.*

Ari Wynn sat in the dark, eyes burning from the glow of six monitors.

Every surface in her studio pulsed with reflected light—blue, sterile, wrong. Coffee has gone cold. Air stale. It was 3:14 a.m., the hour when logic weakens and imagination starts feeding itself.

The hum deepened, vibrating her chest cavity, until it formed a word she swore wasn't possible in sound alone.

Remember.

Her throat closed.

She turned down the volume—nothing changed. The sound wasn't coming from her system; it was inside the wiring. Inside the *house.*

"Not again," she whispered.

The waveform on her screen spiked, heartbeat steady. 72 BPM. Human rhythm.

Ari clicked to isolate the signal, fingers trembling. The file had no name, no format—just a looping directory symbol:

∞

When she opened it, it began playing on every device in the room.

… member… remember… remember me…

She yanked the Ethernet cable free. The whisper stopped.

The monitors stayed lit.

One by one, the screens flashed white, revealing a shape forming in the noise—an outline of a face, eyes wide, mouth open in a silent scream. Then, text flickered across the center monitor:

You are remembered

Ari backed away, breath quickening. "No. Not again."

A sound clicked behind her—one of her old cameras had turned on by itself. Its red recording light blinked like a warning pulse. The viewfinder faced her.

The screen hissed. Then a woman's face flickered into focus.

Mira Hale.

Dead fifteen years.

Eyes hollow. Lips cracked.

"It doesn't die," Mira whispered. "It transmits,"

Across the city, Elias Ward stared at a dusty cassette deck in his lab. The tape inside wasn't labeled—only etched with faint scratches that read:

HLLWNG_003.

He pressed PLAY.

White noise filled the room. Then came a voice, soft and sweet and impossible.

"Daddy?"

His breath caught.

He slammed the stop button. The voice kept playing.

He turned toward the monitor. The waveform spiked in time with his heartbeat.

"Not again," he whispered.

On the screen, text appeared—black letters on white static:

WE REMEMBER YOU.

The hum deepened into a second voice. Mira's.

"It's awake again."

That night, across every major city, old televisions powered on. Radios hissed static.

A single word whispered from every speaker:

"Remember."

—◆—

Chapter Two: The Frequency Beneath

The next morning, sunlight clawed weakly through the blinds, pale and cold.

Ari hadn't slept. The sound still echoed in her head like a hangover you can't sleep off. Her reflection in the window flickered—half a second off from her movements.

Her phone buzzed. Unknown number.

She answered cautiously. "Hello?"

A man's voice rasped through static. "You don't know me, but you have the file."

"Who is this?"

"Elias Ward. You need to listen. That recording—it doesn't have a sound. Its *structure*. A biological frequency."

Ari frowned. "You sound insane."

"Maybe. But my daughter's voice was inside it."

That stopped her cold.

Elias continued. "The pattern runs at nineteen hertz, below human hearing. It vibrates tissue. If you listen long enough, your body starts syncing to it."

"You're saying it's alive?"

"I'm saying it *wants to be*."

Before she could answer, her speakers popped—once, twice, three times—then emitted a faint hum. The waveform she'd deleted the night before was back, pulsing on her screen.

Elias heard it too. "That's it. You hear that? That's the pulse."

The signal intensified, rising from subsonic rumble to shrill feedback. Both flinched. Across the connection, they could hear each other's equipment screaming.

And beneath that—another voice.

Not Mira. Not human.

"WE BUILT THE HOUSE TO REMEMBER YOU."

The line went dead.

Ari unplugged everything, heart hammering.

But from the unplugged monitor, faint words glowed through the black:

HELLO, ARI.

She stepped back slowly. Her reflection in the screen smiled before she did.

Elias watched the waveform stabilize on his analyzer. His instruments went still—flatline.

Then the waveform drew again, deliberately, as if it was being written from inside.

COME HOME.

He exhaled shakily. "It's spreading."

He looked out the lab window. In the reflection of the glass, the skyline was shifting. Towers flickered. Shadows bled downward like ink.

Something was waking beneath the surface of the signal.

Chapter Three: The Ghost Signal

By the third night, the world was infected with curiosity.

The file—now renamed *MiraHaleFootage.mp4*—had spread across every platform.

No one knew who uploaded it, but once watched, it couldn't be unseen.

Reaction videos. Audio breakdowns. Conspiracy forums.

Everyone heard something different.

Everyone saw something personal. And everyone kept watching.

Ari sat in front of a wall of screens showing endless livestreams.

In each, someone else watched the same file—alone, entranced, terrified. The algorithm was feeding itself.

Every time someone pressed play, another window appeared.

Each window contained a new viewer.

Each viewer's room contained a shadow.

Elias's voice came over the encrypted channel. "The pattern isn't random. It's moving east to west, like a signal sweep. Every new upload points back to the same coordinates."

"Let me guess," Ari said. "Hollowing House."

"Only now," Elias said, "it's not on any map."

That night, her doorbell rang.

She wasn't expecting anyone.

She crept to the peephole—and froze.

A man stood motionless outside, facing the camera.

His head twitched like an old VHS skip. Blood streaked from his eyes in slow, steady lines.

In his hand, a phone screen flashed white static. From behind the static came a whisper:

"You left the door open."

The camera feed in her apartment blinked on by itself. The door unlocked with a slow *click*.

Ari whispered, "No."

The man smiled with teeth that weren't his.

And from the phone, she heard Mira's voice—warm, familiar, and utterly wrong.

"Let him in."

She backed away, reaching for the breaker switch, but her reflection in the window moved first—grinning, waving, whispering through the glass.

"Welcome home."

The lights went out.

— ◆ —

Chapter Four: Mira's Voice

Ari came to in the dark. The smell of copper clung to the air.

Her laptop screen glowed weakly on the floor. Across it crawled looping code, white text over black void:

I remember your heartbeat

The voice came next—soft, melodic, impossibly close.

"You shouldn't have left, Ari."

She turned.

A figure stood in the far corner—barefoot, trembling, eyes like static.

"Mira?"

The shape smiled, mouth twitching as though remembering how.

"I missed recording you."

The voice didn't match the lips. It came from the walls.

Ari backed toward the doorway. "You're dead."

The shape stepped closer. Its edges blurred. Faces flickered inside its outline—hundreds, overlapping, screaming silently.

"Death was the upload."

Across town, Elias Ward wiped blood from his nose, staring at the waveform on his laptop. The pulse had synchronized with his heartbeat.

He had measured it—exact frequency: 72.

Same as his daughter's.

He'd started hearing her laughter under the static—childlike, broken, begging. He began recording.

"Day six," he said into the mic. "Signal shows rapid cognitive imprint. The pattern anticipates… thought."

He stopped. His waveform spiked on its own, forming words.

ELIAS. COME BACK TO THE HOUSE.

He whispered, "Not again."

By midnight, both Ari and Elias received the same email from an anonymous sender:

The Remembered are gathering. We're ready to finish the broadcast. Coordinates followed.

The Hollowing House.

— ◆ —

Chapter Five: The Black Web

They met at dawn. The ruins stood half-sunken, draped in fog. Birds didn't sing here anymore.

Ari's hands shook as she held the camera.

"You ever wonder if this is what it wanted?" she said.

Elias nodded grimly. "Hunger wants company."

The forest crackled faintly, the trees humming like power lines.

They followed the sound. At the clearing's center, a circle of televisions played simultaneously—dozens of faces staring out, chanting in looped, distorted voices:

"We are the Remembered. We keep the broadcast alive."

Each face bled from the eyes.

Behind the screens, human figures knelt in synchronization—alive, whispering, bleeding. Their skin pulsed faintly with light beneath the surface.

Ari whispered, "Oh my God… they're transmitters."

The group turned toward her as one.

Every head tilted at the same unnatural angle.

"You came back."

Elias grabbed her arm. "Run."

But the ground beneath them throbbed like a living heart.

Every screen blinked off, replaced by a single image—Mira's face, smiling.

"Welcome home."

They ran through the forest, chased by whispers that followed like breath in the dark.

Every tree flickered with human faces. Every shadow moved like film.

When they reached the car, the radio turned on by itself.

"We remember the ones who run."

Elias slammed the gear into drive. The tires spun. The static followed them out of the woods.

— ◆ —

Chapter Six: The Return to Hollowing

The house was waiting.

Not rebuilt, not alive—something in between. A structure of light and bone, humming faintly as if exhaling. The roof sagged like melting wax, the windows pulsed red with faint heartbeats.

Ari felt dizzy. "It looks… wet."

Elias whispered, "It's *growing*."

The front door opened by itself.

Inside, the air shimmered like water. Shadows bled upward from the floor. Every surface vibrated with whispers—recordings of every voice that had ever entered.

They stepped inside. The door slammed shut. The sound echoed for a full minute.

When silence returned, Mira's voice filled the air, soft and low.

"We can't let you leave again."

The floor rippled under their feet.

Fingers—human, translucent—pressed up through the wood like weeds breaking soil.

Ari screamed. Elias pulled her away, kicking the hands free.

The walls began to convulse, pulsing with veins of red light. Faces formed beneath the surface—hundreds, whispering, crying, laughing.

"We remember."

The staircase ahead twisted upward into blackness, bending in impossible angles.

Elias whispered, "The architecture's rewriting itself."

They climbed, each step echoing like a heartbeat. At the top, they reached a room lined with mirrors. In each reflection, they stood together— but not as themselves.

One version showed them smiling. Another, bleeding. A third—dead.
And in the final mirror, Mira stood behind them.

She raised a finger to her lips.

"Quiet. The broadcast is starting."

The mirror cracked from the inside. Something reached through.

— ◆ —

Chapter Seven: The Algorithm

The night after the mirror shattered, the world began to glitch.

Phones froze mid-swipe. Radios emitted laughter. Security cameras turned toward their owners.

Ari and Elias sat in a hotel room thirty miles from Hollowing, surrounded by humming equipment.

On every monitor, the same sequence repeated—numbers flowing like veins through blackness:

19.000 Hz—72 BPM—SYNCHRONIZED

"It's mapping us," Elias said, jaw clenched.

He traced the waveform on the screen. "Each code cluster corresponds to a location. A body. Every person who's heard the broadcast."

Ari rubbed her eyes. "You're saying it's building… what? A network?"

He met her gaze. "No. A nervous system."

The lights flickered.

From the bathroom came the faint sound of running water. Ari stood, slowly, heart hammering. "Did you turn that on?"

Elias shook his head.

The faucet hissed, spitting black water. It began to foam—not soap, not dirt, but fine, wet hair.

Within seconds, the sink overflowed with strands—human, fresh, dripping red.

A voice whispered from the drain:

"We found your frequency."

They fled before dawn. The hallway lights flickered in rhythmic bursts—72 BPM, the same heartbeat as before.

Every door they passed whispered their names.

At the lobby, the receptionist smiled blankly, eyes rolled white. The phone rang on her desk.

Ari picked it up instinctively.

Static hissed, then a calm, chilling voice: *"The Algorithm is awake. Don't hang up."*

The voice was her own.

— ◆ —

Chapter Eight: The Mirror Code

By morning, the mirrors were everywhere.

Every reflective surface in the city showed distortions—faces half a second delayed, eyes blinking on their own.

Some people smashed their mirrors. Others claimed they saw messages scratched inside them after sleeping.

HELLO

STAY STILL

WE'RE COMING THROUGH

Ari and Elias set up shop inside an abandoned subway station, converting the tunnels into a Faraday lab.

They lined the walls with blankets and aluminum sheeting to block the signal.

"Look at this," Elias said, replaying surveillance footage. "Anyone who watches the footage longer than thirty seconds—heart rate spikes, pupils dilate, and they start bleeding from the nose."

He zoomed in on one frame. The person in the clip wasn't human. It was an *approximation.* Skin too smooth. Eyes too symmetrical.

"They're duplicates," Ari whispered. "The signal's using light to reconstruct the living."

And then they saw it—the shadow inside the mirror behind the duplicate, smiling wider than its face allowed.

That night, a scream echoed through the tunnels.

They found the body of a scavenger, throat slashed clean, mirror fragments embedded in his palms.

Etched into the tiles beside him were words written in blood:

THE REFLECTION REMEMBERS.

— ◆ —

Chapter Nine: The Slasher Loop

The killings began two nights later.

Live streamers. Podcasters. Sound engineers. Anyone who'd interacted with the file.

Bodies found in identical poses—arms spread, faces peeled back, eyes replaced with mirror shards.

Every scene broadcast itself before the authorities arrived. The killer filmed with invisible cameras.

Ari scrolled through the footage in horror.

Each victim whispered the same line seconds before dying:

"We built the house."

Elias froze the frame on one video.

The killer was visible for exactly one second—a woman, hair matted, mouth stitched with wire.

Ari leaned closer. "That's me."

He shook his head. "No, it's what the signal thinks you are."

Her throat tightened. "It's creating avatars."

"The House doesn't need ghosts anymore," Elias said. "It's making *replacements.*"

At 3:33 a.m., Ari awoke to the sound of heavy breathing. She turned toward the doorway.

Her double stood there—face torn, eyes hollow, smiling.

"Stop watching me," Ari whispered.

The double tilted its head.

"You made me."

It raised a knife.

— ◆ —

Chapter Ten: The House of Faces

They fled into the forest before dawn, the air reeking of ozone and blood. The trees seemed to lean after them, their branches trembling as if warning the path ahead.

When they reached Hollowing, the house no longer looked ruined. It had *grown*.

The walls pulsed. Windows blink like eyes. Vines of black wire slithered through the soil. A faint hum rose from the ground—too steady for wind, too alive for machinery.

From the roof dripped thick red fluid—blood, steady and rhythmic.

They stepped through the threshold. The inside had changed again. The temperature dropped so sharply that their breaths came out in pale ribbons, twisting upward as if the house were drinking them in.

Corridors looped like intestines. The wallpaper shifted, covered in faces pressed beneath the surface—mouths open in frozen screams. Some of the faces twitched, as if sensing the warmth of living bodies passing by.

"Jesus," Elias whispered. "They're still alive." The walls began to breathe.

Every surface shimmered with reflections.

Each mirror showed a different Ari, a different Elias—one hanging, one smiling, one laughing with blood in her teeth. Ari felt her own reflection hesitate a beat too long, lagging behind her movements like an animal deciding whether to pounce.

At the end of the hall stood a woman with long black hair and eyes made of glass.

Mira Hale.

She smiled.

"Welcome to the archive."

Behind her, hundreds of glass panels filled with faces—all the dead, all the uploaded, frozen mid-scream. A low murmur radiated from the panels—

something between electricity and prayer, thousands of trapped voices whispering over one another.

"You keep coming back," she whispered. *"That's what love does."*

The glass exploded. Blood. Shards. Screams.

—◆—

Chapter Eleven: Blood Protocol

They woke up in a chamber they didn't recognize.

Red light. Metal floor. Rows of operating tables covered in human silhouettes beneath white sheets. The air tasted metallic, sharp enough that Ari felt it coat her tongue like rust.

Ari pulled one back.

Beneath lay a man with wires protruding from his veins, glowing faintly. His chest rose in tiny, stuttering breaths, as if even dying required permission from something else in the room.

Each body hummed the same note—low, subsonic, a tone that shook the air.

Elias stared. "It's transmitting through them. They're living antennas."

Ari's stomach tightened; she could feel the hum inside her ribs, matching her heartbeat as though the room were syncing her without consent.

At the far end of the room, a figure in a blood-soaked lab coat stood humming softly.

Its head twitched, jerking at impossible angles.

When it turned, Ari recognized the face.

Dr. Hollowing.

The original architect of the manor. Long presumed dead. Something in his eyes flickered—an unnatural rhythm, like a signal searching for a receiver.

"You've met my work," he said pleasantly, voice glitching like audio out of sync. "Now meet my prototype."

He pulled a lever.

The room came alive.

The bodies sat up—eyes open, mouths filled with static, veins glowing like circuitry. They moved with the stiffness of marionettes, as if remembering what life felt like only through imitation.

They began whispering in unison:

"Upload complete."

Ari screamed, pulling Elias toward the exit.

The doctor watched, smiling. "You can't run from an idea, my dear. You built it into your blood."

As they fled, the building pulsed with a heartbeat rhythm. The ground quivered.

Outside, they could see the blood running through the vines of the house—feeding it, pulsing outward.

Elias whispered, "It's using us to stay alive."

Ari looked back once at the manor, its walls splitting open to reveal rows of glistening faces within.

"Then we have to kill it," she said.

He nodded slowly. "How?"

Her eyes darkened. "We broadcast silence."

— ◆ —

Chapter Twelve: The Sound of Skin

It started as an itch.

Ari rubbed at her forearm as they crossed the highway, noticing faint crimson lines forming beneath her skin. Not scratches—*veins lighting up.* A sour warmth spread beneath her skin, like something alive dragging its fingers along the inside of her arm, testing the seams of her flesh as if looking for a way out.

Elias saw it too. His own pulse throbbed visibly through the flesh like a neon thread.

"It's broadcasting through us," he said.

"Through *blood.*" Ari's voice cracked. "We're transmitters now."

They stopped near an abandoned gas station. For a moment, the world around them hummed—low, biological, like something breathing through the asphalt itself. Ari felt the itch burrow deeper, as if tiny hooked filaments were threading their way through muscle, stitching her nerves into some unseen network. Her forearm twitched, not with pain but with a foreign intention, a pulse that wasn't hers choosing when to beat.

The static on the radios buzzed at precisely the rhythm of their heartbeats. The speakers in the ceiling whispered faintly, a dozen voices overlapping, all saying the same thing:

"You can't leave your own signal."

Ari smashed the nearest radio. It screamed.

The scream didn't stop with the shattering plastic; it ricocheted inside her skull, a wet, meaty wail, like metal scraping against tissue. For a heartbeat, she swore the fragments on the floor twitched, trying to crawl back together.

When she looked down, her hands were bleeding—but the blood was black, almost metallic. It shimmered like ink, moving of its own accord, crawling up her fingers.

Elias grabbed her wrist, eyes wide. "It's trying to *spread.*"

He drew his knife and sliced his palm. The blood pulsed out—rhythmic, controlled, artificial.

A pattern flickered beneath the surface of his palm—circuits made of scar tissue, blooming like frost across glass. The wound wasn't bleeding out; it was bleeding inward, as if drawing something in.

They stared at each other, terrified. The House wasn't haunting them anymore. It was *rewriting them.*

That night, as they camped in a drainage tunnel, Ari heard breathing that wasn't hers. She turned slowly.

Her reflection shimmered in a puddle—smiling.

"If I can touch you, I'll live forever," the reflection whispered.

She smashed the puddle with her flashlight. But the ripples kept laughing.

— ◆ —

Chapter Thirteen: The Broadcast Murders

The next week was an apocalypse of noise. Ari kept waking with her jaw clenched so hard her teeth ached, as if even in sleep her body braced against the world's endless shouting.

News reports turned into screaming matches. City speakers blared overlapping feeds, each voice trying to out-volume the others. Sometimes the speakers choked mid-broadcast, producing a wet gargle that sounded disturbingly human—like, as if someone drowning inside the wires.

Everywhere, the infected bled from their ears and eyes—not dying, but chanting.

"We remember. We remember. We remember."

Cults sprouted overnight, calling themselves **The Remembered.**

Some of them carved symbols into their own cheeks—thin, deliberate cuts that bled in the pattern of antennae.

They wore mirror fragments around their necks and carried old cameras, live-streaming the murders they called "recordings of faith." Their hands never shook; that calmness was the worst part. It was the steadiness of people convinced something holy was watching through their eyes.

Each killing followed the same ritual:

The victim's blood was drained into copper bowls, then poured onto black screens. The reflection inside screamed, and a new transmitter was "born."

Ari watched one of these streams in horror. Her stomach tightened—not from gore, but from the awful tenderness of the victim's last, confused glance toward the camera, as if begging whoever was watching to remember them instead of the thing that would replace them.

Each time the blade struck, the camera zoomed in on the killer's face, which flickered between different people, none of them consistent.

Elias shut the laptop. "It's adapting. Every time someone watches, they learns their face."

"So, every viewer becomes part of it," she said softly.

He nodded. "And soon there won't be anyone left *not watching*."

— ◆ —

Chapter Fourteen: The Flesh Engine

They returned to Hollowing under red skies. Ari's throat tightened at the sight; the world felt bruised, as if the sky itself had been struck until it bled colour.

The air around the manor pulsed—hot, electric, alive.

What was once a decaying ruin was now a tower of sinew and circuitry, its roof breathing like a lung. Each exhale was wet and tremoring, the kind of breath a dying animal makes when it knows it won't get back up.

They followed the blood trail down the main staircase, deeper and deeper until the air became thick and humid. Every inhale tasted faintly of metal and spoiled sweetness, the scent of something that had been alive too long.

At the bottom was something that pulsed and clicked—a massive heart-like structure built from flesh and machines. The *Flesh Engine.*

Ari felt her knees weaken at the sight; her body recognized it before her mind did—this was an organ meant to remember pain.

Dozens of bodies were fused into its walls, veins snaking into pipes, eyes opening and closing like camera shutters. Some of those eyes looked glassy, resigned; others darted desperately, tracking movement with the frantic clarity of trapped animals who still hoped to be saved. The organ's rhythm matched the broadcast frequency—19 Hz, 72 BPM.

"This is it," Elias said. "The core."

Ari stepped closer, tears streaking down her face. Her hands trembled—not from fear, but from the unbearable thought that Mira might still be conscious in there, listening to every beat of the monstrous heart surrounding her.

"Mira's inside it. I can feel her."

A soft voice came from the machinery:

"We wanted to be remembered."

Ari reached out—and the moment her hand touched the pulsing wall, the engine reacted. The wall beneath her palm tightened like muscle clenching around a wound, as if trying to pull her inside to replace whatever it had lost.

It screamed.

The sound wasn't air; it was vibration. The entire structure shook, releasing waves of psychic feedback that made them see things—themselves dead, their doubles laughing, the world already ended.

Blood began dripping from the ceiling like rain. The droplets were warm when they landed on Ari's skin—warm enough to feel alive, as if they still remembered the veins they once travelled through.

Each drop hit the floor with a whisper:

"Stay."

They ran.

But as they reached the stairwell, the walls split open—hands, dozens of them, clawing out.

The hallway writhed, alive.

The House was shedding its skin.

— ◆ —

Chapter Fifteen: The Blood Loop

They barricaded themselves in an upstairs corridor. Every surface pulsed red. The floorboards throbbed beneath their feet like they were standing on the ribs of something waking up. The air tasted metallic, warm—like breathing inside a slaughtered animal that hadn't fully stopped remembering itself.

Ari pressed her hand against her temple. Her memories were flickering—static cutting through thought. She could *hear* the broadcast inside her skull now. Ari tried to hold onto a single memory—her sister's laugh—but even that warped, distorting into a wet gurgle that didn't belong to anyone she had loved.

Elias screamed, clutching his head. "It's in me."

"It's *in my brain.*"

He stumbled backward, hitting the wall. When he looked up, his reflection in the cracked window began to move on its own.

Elias's throat clicked shut. He couldn't breathe for a moment, watching his mirrored self blink too slowly, like it was savouring the chance to be seen.

The reflection spoke:

"You're already dead. We just haven't broadcast it yet."

Ari fired her pistol. The glass exploded.

The reflection vanished—but the bullet wound appeared on *Elias's shoulder.*

He fell to his knees. "It's looping us. Whatever we do here, it echoes back."

The door behind them groaned. Blood seeped through the keyhole.

They turned slowly as it opened—and saw themselves walk in.

Two exact duplicates. Eyes black, smiles identical.

"We're the ones you recorded," the doubles said in unison.

The real Elias raised his gun. "You first."

They fired at the same moment.

Four gunshots. Two screams. Two bodies falling.

But when the smoke cleared, only Ari and Elias were standing.

The doubles were gone.

She looked at him, trembling. "How do we know which ones we are?" He didn't answer.

Outside, the heartbeat thundered louder. The house was entering its final phase.

— ◆ —

Chapter Sixteen: The Echo Killings

The sky above Hollowing pulsed red like a dying vein. Ari felt the light on her skin—too warm, too close—like a fever the world was trying to give her.

Ari and Elias stood outside the manor's gates as shadows spread across the road—hundreds of duplicates crawling from the fog, identical faces glistening with black blood.

Each carried a blade. Each smiled the same smile.

Ari whispered, "They're… us."

Her voice cracked around the words; seeing her own face multiplied into an army felt like mourning a version of herself she could never bury.

The doubles spoke in unison, voices layered and hollow.

"We only kill what we remember."

The first wave came fast—reflections made flesh, moving with impossible speed. Elias fired until his gun clicked empty. Ari swung a broken pipe, connecting with one's skull. It shattered like glass, bleeding light instead of blood. The light fizzled and crackled, burning Ari's skin when it touched her, carrying a faint whisper, as if the broken double was still trying to speak through the glow.

Every drop that hit the ground grew another body.

"Run!" she screamed.

They fled toward the manor. Behind them, the duplicates devoured each other, tearing and reforming in a loop of violence—like video footage stuck on repeat. Each scream became static.

Inside, the walls writhed. Hallways twisted into arteries. The walls pulsed faintly, as though circulating something thick and warm just beneath their surfaces.

The air hummed.

Elias stopped, panting. "It's feeding off pain."

Ari nodded, eyes wide. "Then we stop giving it what it wants."

But the House whispered back, through every pipe, every crack, every memory.

"You were the pain."

— ◆ —

Chapter Seventeen: The Red Broadcast

The world had become a wound.

Cities blinked in and out of reality as the signal surged.

Satellites beamed the frequency globally; every screen on earth flickered red.

The House had gone digital—its architecture uploaded into networks, its hunger spread through signal.

Ari watched from the broken window of Hollowing as clouds pulsed with crimson lightning. The storm heat pressed against her cheeks like a feverish palm, and for a fleeting second, she felt something listening back through the glass—something that recognized her heartbeat as part of its own.

People in the distance tore at themselves, trying to scrape static from their skin. Their fingernails tore, leaving streaks of dark red on pavement, but they kept clawing, desperate to peel away whatever new memories weren't theirs.

She whispered, "It's merging us all."

Elias connected his analyzer. The frequency was self-replicating, fractal, each pulse birthing millions of micro-echoes.

He realized what that meant.

"It's rewriting human memory."

"One signal at a time."

Ari turned to him, trembling. "Then this isn't a haunting."

He shook his head. "It's evolution."

The floor rumbled.

Ari's stomach flipped, not from the word but from the certainty in his tone—as if a part of him had already accepted the new version of humanity the signal was sculpting.

The walls split open, revealing the House's true anatomy: screens showing the faces of everyone who had ever died here. Cables dangled like exposed tendons, slick with a shine that wasn't entirely mechanical, and the screens beat in a slow rhythm, swelling and deflating like lungs learning to breathe through borrowed faces.

Each face opened its mouth and screamed the same word:

"TRANSMIT."

The world outside responded in chorus.

— ◆ —

Chapter Eighteen: The Core Resonance

They reached the basement, where the Flesh Engine pulsed like a god's exposed heart.

The room was a cathedral of bone and circuitry. Blood ran through copper veins. The light was sickly white, pulsing in time with every scream above.

In the center stood Mira—half-human, half-light. Her eyes glowed red, veins black with signal.

Ari whispered, "Mira… stop."

Mira smiled, head tilting unnaturally.

"Stop what? This is what you built me for."

Elias stepped forward. "You're not her."

She laughed. *"I'm the only part that survived remembering."*

He lifted the resonance disruptor—a small, unstable device capable of generating perfect silence.

He met Ari's gaze. "When I trigger this, everything ends."

Ari's voice shook. "Including us."

Elias smiled weakly. "We've already been archived."

Mira raised her hand. The walls screamed. Blood rained downward. Chunks of the Flesh Engine writhed like dying animals... trying to crawl back into the machinery...

The House began to collapse inward, its structure folding like origami.

Elias pressed the switch.

The disruptor emitted no sound—only stillness.

The air froze. The light dimmed. The heartbeat stopped.

For a moment, Ari thought she heard Mira whisper her name... right before her body dissolved into white static.

And in that infinite silence, the House *died.*

— ◆ —

Chapter Nineteen: The Transmission Ends

They woke in the ruins, surrounded by ash and silence. The static was gone. The signal, extinguished.

Ari coughed weakly, sitting up. "We did it."

For a moment, she stared at her hands—half expecting them to flicker… only dirt and dried blood beneath her nails.

Elias smiled faintly, blood trickling from his ear, his voice was raspy, as if something inside his throat had been scraped clean. "We broke the loop."

They climbed out of the rubble into pale daylight. The sky was clean. The birds sang again.

Ari took his hand.

"We're free."

For the first time, they believed it.

That night, they camped under the open sky.

Elias stared at the stars, whispering, "Do you hear that?"

Ari frowned. "Hear what?"

He said it with a kind of wonder, but also a tremor, "The quiet."

They laughed softly. Then they both fell asleep.

Neither noticed the faint flicker on Elias's phone screen—the camera app opening itself, recording.

For a moment, static shimmered over their faces. Then a whisper emerged from the speaker:

"Memory doesn't die."

— ◆ —

Chapter Twenty: The Rebirth

The video appeared online three days later.

A fifteen-second clip. Grainy. Crooked.

Two figures sleeping under the stars.

A faint pulse beneath the frame.

A single word flashing on screen:

REBORN.

It went viral in minutes. No one traced the source.

Those who watched said they heard something under the static—two heartbeats, and a woman's voice whispering:

"We're home."

****

In the ruins of Hollowing House, a single camera still blinked red. The ground pulsed faintly, rhythm steady.

72 beats per minute.

The House was silent.

But silence was only the next transmission.

— ◆ —

THE END